HAWTHORN
& CHILD

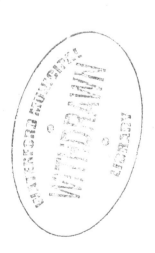

HAWTHORN & CHILD

Keith Ridgway

GRANTA

Granta Publications, 12 Addison Avenue, London W11 4QR

First published in Great Britain by Granta Books, 2012

Earlier versions of 'Goo Book' and 'Rothko Eggs' appeared in the *New Yorker* and *Zoetrope: All-Story* respectively.

A CIP catalogue record for this book is available from the British Library

10 9 8 7 6 5 4 3 2 1

ISBN 978 1 84708 526 9 (hardback)
ISBN 978 1 84708 741 6 (trade paperback)

Typeset in Minion by Patty Rennie

Printed and bound by CPI Group (UK) Ltd, Croydon, CR0 4YY

For Jasper

and with thanks to my family, especially my father
W. J. Ridgway; Raj Sonecha; David Miller and
Alex Goodwin; Philip Gwyn Jones; John Self;
Cressida Leyshon; David Hayden;
and Seán McGovern.

1934

He dreamed he was sleeping, and Child was driving. Driving but not moving. He was sleeping on the passenger seat and Child wrestled with the wheel, but the car was still. It was the city that was moving. It was dark. The city rushed past them like words on a screen, and he would have read them but they went too fast. He was filled with sorrow. It trickled through him and filled his eyes. He wept and he didn't know why, and he was embarrassed by it but he could not stop. He cried so much that his face disappeared. He dreamed that the siren was on, and it was so loud that it woke him.

He awoke. Child was driving. The city was still and they rushed through it. That was the difference. A finger across a page, taking corners not turning them, hopping little hills, drawing zigzag ciphers on the wide, empty intersections.

His shoulder was pressed into the door and pulled away from it and he touched his seat belt. He had an erection. He wiped at his eyes. Child was smiling at the road. He wouldn't drive like this at any other time of the day. He wouldn't be able to.

– Has he run?

As soon as he'd said it the stupidity of the idea roared back at him. Mishazzo. Running.

Child glanced at him and laughed.

– Shot fired off Seven Sisters, he shouted.

He didn't quite believe him, such was his grin and his mouthing of the corners, gleeful as a roller-coaster. He looked around for something to indicate official business, permission, and shook his head violently, trying to get the sleep to go. He sat up, and was pressed down again. He looked at his crotch. His chin was wet. He saw the radio, and only when he saw it did he hear it, feeding them information in short regular bursts, calm and close together. He couldn't understand them. Their pattern indicated some sort of emergency, declared, somewhere or other.

– What? he asked the radio.

Child said something that he couldn't hear. The streets were deserted. What time was it? There was next to no traffic. Why was the siren on? He switched it off.

– Someone needs to do bad before we can do good.

– Shot fired. That it?

– One male injured. Local unit just arrived. Ambulance arrived. Shot fired from car. Armed response imminent. Rivers raised from his bed. All hands on deck! Scramble! Scramble!

Child was cackling at the footpaths, leering at the kerbs.

– Finally we get to do something other than sit on our arses.

2

He tried to manage his arms. They wanted to stretch but they were tensed up against the roll of the car. In his dream there had been ghosts as well, he thought. Around the car. Small dark ghosts with wings and muscles. Flapping. He became aware of a pain in his neck. And a headache. He opened the window an inch. Two inches. Ghosts like little birds, tough little tattooed birds. Bad things. His erection began to subside.

They turned a corner somewhere near Wood Green, into the cold canyon of the shopping street. Child punched the siren as they passed some taxis and a pedestrian crossing. He drove with his glasses slipped to the end of his nose and his head thrown back so that he could see through them.

– What?

Child was muttering.

– It's near where I used to live, he shouted. With Amy. When I lived with Amy.

– What is?

– Hampley Road.

– Hampley?

– Road. Scene of the crime. Stick your head out the window or something.

He stared at the clock and looked at his watch and fumbled in his pocket, and then couldn't remember what he was fumbling for. Five twenty-nine. 0529. 5.29 a.m. Shot fired, Hampley Road, Finsbury Park, man injured. He wasn't fumbling, he was fixing his cock.

– Why are we going this way?

Some people stepped away from a car as they passed. Three men, one woman, maybe more, young maybe, he couldn't see, scattering as they passed, and he turned in his seat and watched them re-form into a group in the middle of the road and stare after them, and he kept on looking backwards even after Child had turned another corner and there was nothing more to see because he liked the way the stretch in his back and his chest and his shoulders made him feel. It eased his headache and it pinched the pain in his neck. He yawned again and listened to the radio, monotone, scripted. You fire a gun in this city and certain things inevitably follow. Hampley Road. Armed response on scene. Ambulance off scene. Victim off scene.

He was awake.

– We're going the wrong way, he shouted. Child looked at him. The siren wasn't on. The shout had sounded insane.

– We're not going to Hampley Road, Hawthorn. We're going to the hospital.

He was in his twenties and his hands were slick with blood. Then a nurse was wiping them with a cloth and they became a faded pinking, stuck in the air, his arms bent at the elbow for no reason, flapping a little. For no reason. Not flapping. Turning at the wrist, like a sock-puppet show stripped naked and scalded, doing a little dumb show over the prone body on the table. He was a body on a table. Weight of flesh and bone.

Wound and contusion. Half a dozen people gathered around him with what you would swear was ill intent, such was the way they shouted and darted and snapped. They poked and peered at the body. They tubed the body and they hooked it up. They shifted and bound the body. They cut and pressed and injected the body. They worked on it as if furious.

Hawthorn was sweating and cold.

– Lay your arms down, Daniel, that's it, lay them down. Daniel? Daniel! Put your arms down for me darling, that's it.

– Move please.

Early twenties, average build. He was moaning and shockingly alive, and his socks were still on his feet, and there were drops of blood, splatters, on his legs somehow, his bare legs, raw looking. His underpants too, still clinging to him, but halfway down his thighs, where they'd been pushed or pulled. His genitals looked out of place, as if they were the last thing you'd expect to find on a naked body. The rest of his clothes had been cut from him and lay in a sodden heap on a side table. All the attention was focused on his stomach, his abdomen, around there somewhere. Hawthorn tried not to see too much.

Child moved over to look at the clothes. Hawthorn stood off to the right, glancing at the discarded bloody things that littered the floor – bits of bandages and padding from the ambulance, yellow needle caps, little torn open packages.

– Move, please.

– Can't get at it there.

– All right, Daniel. Don't move if you can.

– Move, please.

– Watch it. Clamp . . . pack here. Here.

He shrieked. Daniel. A short painful burst of non words, and his arms were up again, and Hawthorn found himself looking suddenly for his face.

– OK, Daniel, OK, easy. That's the worst of it. The pain will ease now. Daniel? You OK, Daniel?

His face was smeared in blood. His chest was covered in bits and pieces. They were using it as a table. His eyes were opening and closing. His mouth was making shapes.

– OK, he said. OK OK OK. OK.

Child reappeared.

– Can I ask him a few things?

– He's going straight to surgery.

– Hang on, said a nurse.

– Daniel? I'm police.

– Hang on, I said.

Hawthorn had his notebook in his hand. He looked at it. He rummaged for a pen. Child was leaning over the boy's head.

– Daniel, can you remember what happened? Can you tell us what happened?

– I was shot.

One of the nurses laughed.

– Do you know who shot you?

They were moving around him faster now, taping things to

his arms, cleaning, wiping patches of his skin with pads and cloths. A nurse was cutting away his underpants. On his hips there was padding, bandages, a hand holding things in place. There was a smell of sweat and blood and piss. They covered his lower body with a sort of paper sheet.

– A car. Shot me.

– What kind of car?

– Old car.

His voice was full of hard breathing but it was clear. His hair was damp. One of his eyes was bloodshot. His skin was a horrible white. There was a dark bruise coming up on his left shoulder. He looked around them, around their heads and at the ceiling behind them. Then his eyes fixed on Hawthorn's eyes and stayed there.

– Daniel? What do you mean old? Like an old banger?

– No. Old-fashioned.

He looked at Hawthorn. As if he thought it was Hawthorn who was talking to him.

– Do you mean a vintage car?

– Vintage. Yeah. OK. Came along. Side me.

– Did you see who was driving?

– No.

– Did you see anyone in the car?

– No.

They took the brakes off the trolley.

– That's all I'm afraid. We have to get him to surgery. Right now.

– What colour was it, Daniel?

– Dark. Black or . . . dark. Sideboards. Not sideboards. At the side . . .

– Running boards?

– Running boards.

They began to move him. He looked straight up. At the ceiling and the lights.

– A beautiful old car came out of nowhere and shot me.

Hawthorn called in. Frank Lenton was running the office.

– A vintage car?

– With running boards. Dark. Possibly black. Dark, anyway.

– Number plate?

– No.

– Model?

– No.

– A black vintage car with running boards.

– There can't be very many driving around at 5 a.m. on a Monday morning, Frank. Don't sound so glum.

They had the place to themselves. Child had put on a pair of latex gloves. He opened the wallet that sat beside the clothes. Hawthorn held the phone out towards him.

– Credit card, Daniel Field. F-I-E-L-D. Debit card. Work photo ID. IFM Banking. City. 38 Cellar Street. Echo charlie 3. 4 yankee delta. Oyster card. Nectar card. Tesco Club card. Virgin Active gym card. Boots card. Café Out loyalty card. Tea Smith loyalty card. Two twenty-pound notes and one ten.

Three first-class stamps. Business cards, various, blah blah, not his. No driver's licence. No address.

There was silence on the phone. Hawthorn put it on speaker and set it down on the table. Child was going through the clothes, shaking his head. Charcoal suit, white shirt, tie, light raincoat, black shoes.

– There's no phone here.

– No phone, Frank.

There was a pause, then a crackle.

– There's one at the scene.

– Whose scene?

– Rivers is on his way. Lowry and Clarke are there now. Give me one of the numbers. The credit card.

Hawthorn leaned over the card and called out the numbers.

– Is he dead then?

– He's gone to surgery.

– Right. Daniel Field. 16 Nestor Lane, N-E-S-T-O-R. L-A-N-E. November 4, 4 echo alpha. D.O.B. twenty-eight, nine, nineteen eighty-seven.

Hawthorn wrote. A nurse came back into the room.

– Where do you want us, Frank?

– No idea. Hang on.

The nurse started cleaning up. She ignored them. Child looked at her.

– Will he make it?

She shook her head.

– Don't know. Depends what they find in him. How much blood he lost.

Hawthorn picked up his phone, took it off speaker, held it to his ear.

– Looked like he lost a lot.

– Nah. Internal bleeding will kill him, you know? But maybe. From the way he was talking, moving, that's a good sign. He was not very weak.

Frank crackled back in his ear.

– You were at the . . . Mishazzo thing. You on that?

– Yeah.

– Hang on.

– How long will he be in there?

– I don't know. A long time probably.

He looked at her hands.

– OK, Mishazzo is covered, said Frank. You stay there. Wait to hear from Rivers.

They went looking for the paramedics who had brought him in. They were mopping out the back of the ambulance.

– Did he say anything?

– He said 'What the fuck happened?' a couple of times. He kept on saying 'I've been shot' like he couldn't believe it. And he mentioned a car.

– Did he say what kind of car?

– No. I asked 'Who shot you?' and he said 'A car'.

– Nothing else?

– Nope.

– Do you think he'll make it?

– Nope.

They went to the hospital café. It was too early apparently for anything hot to eat. They had cling-filmed sandwiches and risked the coffee. They sat against a wall, side by side, Child between tables with his legs crossed. He cleaned his glasses and watched Hawthorn.

– Sandwich is yesterday's. Dry.

– Try the coffee.

Hawthorn tried the coffee.

– It's all right.

Child took a sip and made a face.

– Café Out, he said.

– Yeah.

– Is that a gay thing?

– Yeah.

– So he's gay?

– It's a café. They do nice cakes. I wouldn't assume.

– Well, did that look like gay cock to you?

Hawthorn looked at Child seriously for a moment, and said nothing. Child chewed and looked back.

– Who drives vintage cars? he asked, firing crumbs at the air. I'll tell you who. Creepy old queens in cravats. Living in creepy old mansions in Hampstead. You know, with the dungeon.

Hawthorn smiled.

– Young Daniel's broken someone's heart, said Child.

– The dungeon?

– The dungeon.

Hawthorn shook his head.

They watched a man wipe tables. He wore his hair in a net.

– When he wakes up, Hawthorn said. He watched himself use his fork for emphasis. *If* he wakes up. We need to get a better description. We need to get an artist in. Do we have a car artist?

Child laughed.

– Do we have a car artist?

– Yeah.

– I don't know. We'll find that out. Tell Rivers we need a car artist.

Hawthorn yawned and his eyes filled up. He stopped. Stared at the table. He carefully closed his eyes. Opened them again. It was just the yawn. He thought. After a moment. He blinked a couple of times. Cleared his throat. Sipped the coffee. Child was talking.

– Rolls Royce Silver Shadow. An actor or something. Sixties pop star. I should have had juice. I feel like a bag of shit. You need to watch that eye rubbing thing. You already look like someone's poked you with a pair of fingers. I want a bed. You think they have empty beds here somewhere? Unlikely, isn't it? Unlikely.

*

Hawthorn called John Lowry.

– Do you have his phone?

– Yeah. What's all this about a vintage car?

– Vintage car. It's what he said. Old car. With running boards. Pulled up beside him. Shot him. That's all he knows.

– Is he sober?

– He's a banker. On his way to work. What's it look like there?

Child was at the counter negotiating free coffee refills. Hawthorn watched him.

– Useless. It's towards the end of the road, where it meets the main road. He's been walking on the footpath, left hand side of the road, coming up to the crossroads, he's passed the parked cars, into the clearway. There's a bullet in the wall, they're getting that now. Very small calibre, looks like. So we have . . . at least two shots. We have ear witnesses going up to five, but you know what that's like. No eyes. He's left a shoulder bag, with a computer and stuff in it. So, it's no robbery. He's dropped the phone as he fell, either out of his hand or his pocket. No weapon, no shell cases. Cold road. Looks light to me, apart from the bullet. A banker?

– Yeah.

– Well fuck knows then. CCTV is killing good policing. Rivers is here, talk later. Oh. Hang on.

Hawthorn looked at his phone. It was filthy, covered in a film of grease. Dirt clogged the sockets. A patch of some sticky unidentifiable substance adhered to its screen. Child was coming back to the table with two coffees.

– Hawthorn?

– Yes.

– Rivers.

– Morning, sir.

– He's tripping, isn't he?

– I don't think so.

– He's in surgery now?

– Yes, sir. No one seems to know if he'll make it.

– Did he actually say *vintage*?

– He said *old* and *old-fashioned*. Child offered him *vintage* and he took it, like it was the word he'd been looking for. He was specific about running boards, unprompted.

Rivers was quiet for a moment.

– There's that Chrysler thing. It has sort of fake running boards. Well. OK. If that's what we've got then that's what we've got. The Good Samaritan who stopped and called it in is a Mr Jetters. I'm sending him to Highbury. Go down there and get a statement from him. Stay in touch with the hospital though. There's a uniform on the way for presence, but I want you back there as soon as he's out of surgery.

Alan Jetters was a thin man in his forties with blood on his shirt. They found him in reception, pacing. He was in a hurry, he said. He needed to get to work. But he was full of adrenaline and really he wanted to talk. Hawthorn apologized for keeping him, shook his hand, introduced Child, offered him tea. He didn't want tea. They found a room on the second floor. Child went off to the toilet. Hawthorn took off his jacket, glanced at the machine.

– We'll just wait for Detective Child to get back.

– Does he get a lot of ribbing?

– What's that?

– Child. Over his name.

– Oh, ribbing. A little. Yes. I suppose he does. I've stopped noticing really.

– That's not good for a policeman.

– No.

– To stop noticing.

– No.

Hawthorn sat at the table writing things in his notebook.

Child came back. Hawthorn fiddled with the machine, then moved out of the way to let Child do it. The building was overheated. He thought about bullets and cold and Daniel Field's red hands, pink hands, stuck in the air. He missed the cold.

– Is this going to take long? Jetters asked. I'm late for work.

– So is Daniel Field, said Child.

There was a silence, in which Child, turning away from the machine, shot Hawthorn a wink. Then they were all sitting, and the little lights were green.

– He died?

– No, not yet. He's in surgery. His condition is very serious.

– I didn't know his name. I asked him, but I couldn't make

out . . . Anyway. I'm happy to be of whatever help I can. Of course.

They got him to say his name, his address, his date of birth. They said their names.

– Can you just tell us, Hawthorn said, everything that happened, from the beginning?

He offered too much detail. He told them about his usual morning routine, about the slight differences there had been that morning. He told them his route to work, what was on the radio, what the weather was like, how he'd felt, what he was wearing. He was fascinated by the fact that he had guessed that the gunshot was a gunshot as soon as he'd heard it, even though he knew nothing about guns and had never been near one, apart from a go at clay pigeon shooting on a weekend away once, and he hadn't liked that, because he was no good at it, and found those sorts of organized work outings quite awkward. And so on.

Hawthorn wrote things down.

He had been approaching the turn from Almond Road on to Hampley Road when he'd heard it. The first thing he saw when he turned the corner was Daniel Field on the ground. He had driven over to him, pulled in and gone to help.

– He was writhing. Half shouting. Half shouting and half crying. He seemed in terrible pain. He was clutching his stomach, he had his hands pressed to his stomach, but there was blood seeping through his fingers.

Hawthorn wrote down *seeping*. It occurred to him that it was the wrong word.

Jetters had taken off the scarf he'd been wearing and used it instead. Then he'd called 999.

– Did he say anything?

– He kept saying *fuck*. And not much more I'm afraid. A lot of groaning. He seemed to pass out for a moment – and when he opened his eyes he said *What happened?* but that was all.

– You talked to him.

– Yes. I jabbered. I don't know what I said. A lot of nonsense I imagine. *You'll be alright. Hold on. Ambulance is coming.* That kind of thing.

– Did he look at you?

– Yes. Yes he did. When I first arrived he looked me in the eye, and I think for a moment he wondered if I was . . . if I was there to do him harm. He looked scared of me. Perhaps he was just scared anyway. But when I made it clear that I was there to help he didn't look at me so much.

– Can you tell us anything, any half words, anything that sounded like words, that he said? That you can remember.

– Well. I asked what had happened. *What happened?* And he said *car*. And I asked, *Someone in a car?* and he nodded. It was only then that I thought of the possibility of them coming back. I mean, it was, I was . . . it's strange how the mind works. I had seen him, and I had known, somehow, that he had been shot, and I had stopped and gone to help without really thinking about it, and it was only when he said *car* that I

17

thought *uh-oh*, and I realized that they might come back – that someone had actually *shot* him, someone had tried to *kill* him, and that they might still be around, and that I was possibly in some sort of danger.

He shifted in his seat slightly, cleared his throat.

– No one came back, though?

– No. No one. I started to look over my shoulder a little, after that. I asked him what type of car. He said *ochre*.

– Ochre?

– Ochre.

– Are you sure?

– Yes.

Hawthorn looked at Child. He was grinning.

– Do you think he might have said *old car*?

– Old car?

– Old car.

Jetters shrugged.

– Yes, I suppose so. Old car, ochre. Yes. It could have been old car.

Hawthorn wrote for a while but Child kept silent.

– What else?

– What else did he say? I don't think he did say anything else, much. I'm not sure he was trying to say anything. Apart from the couple of questions I asked him, it was just groans and cries and squeals, if I can say that. Extreme pain I imagine. Lots of *Gods* and *Christs*. Though some of that may have been me. He was puffing and blowing. Shivering. He was terribly cold. It was cold there. Dark. Cold and damp and miserable really. I remember thinking that it would be a terrible place to die. I took off my jumper after a while. Partly to help with the pressure, but also because he was so cold.

– There are street lights there. Aren't there?

– It's shadowy, rather than dark, I suppose. There are lamp-posts, yes. He was about midway between lamp-posts. There are pools of light, pools of shadow.

Hawthorn wrote down *pools of light / pools of shadow*.

– When you turned into Hampley Road, did you see anything else?

Jetters coughed. Cleared his throat.

– There was a car. I didn't mention it earlier. It went out of my mind for some reason. And it's very vague now. It was at the junction with Plume Road, leaving Hampley Road. It was there, and I saw it, but I didn't really look at it, if you see what I mean. My attention was on him. On Mr Field. I saw lights I think. Brake lights perhaps, as if it paused at the junction, and then it was gone.

– Which way?

– I'm not entirely certain. I couldn't swear on it, but I have the impression now, I'm not sure why, that it turned to the right into Plume Road.

– North.

– Is it? Yes, you're right. North.

– How would you describe it?

– The car?

– The car, yes.

– Just a shape really. The back of a car. You know. The idea of a car. I think there were brake lights. But you know I'm not even sure of that. But some kind of light or lights. Tail lights or a registration plate light or something. Some kind of shape around that.

– You couldn't see a registration?

– No no. Nothing like that. Nothing so clear. I'm guessing. I don't really know. It was the suggestion of a car, you know. The idea of a car.

Hawthorn looked at Child again. But he just looked back.

– Were the lights high or low?

Jetters looked confused.

– Were they at the standard saloon car height, or were they raised, like on a four-wheel drive for example? Or low down like a sports car?

– Oh I see. I don't know. I don't even know if there were lights. Standard, I suppose. It didn't register. Not noticeably high or low.

– Square lights? Round? Oval?

He shrugged.

– As I say. I am even doubtful as to lights. Shapes of lights is beyond me. Sorry.

– That's OK. This is very helpful.

– Could you hear it? asked Child.

He paused.

– Yes. I think so. Yes, I could, of course. It accelerated off from the junction. It was loud. I heard the engine roar. Well, not roar perhaps. But I certainly heard the engine. It accelerated away. It sounded . . . well, louder, I suppose, than I'd . . . louder than you'd expect. I think. Maybe it was just because there was no other traffic around.

– Can you describe the sound? Smooth? Irregular? High pitched?

– It was a rumble, I think. Like a . . . I don't know. A low rumble. I can't quite recall.

They let him think about it for a while.

– Like?

– Oh I don't know. I really can't remember.

– Were there other cars? To the left of you for example, as you came out on to Hampley Road?

– There were parked cars.

– I mean moving cars.

– I didn't look to the left. I don't think. I don't recall looking to the left. I suppose I must have, when I turned the corner, instinctively, to check. But I don't remember. And I don't remember seeing any other cars. Not then.

– Where there other cars after that?

There were other cars after that. Some of them had made Alan Jetters nervous. None had stopped. One was a *very pale gold.*

– Though I suppose it could have been silver, reflecting my amber hazard lights.

– When did you put them on?

– When I stopped. When I pulled in. I actually don't remember doing it, but they were on all the time, I was aware of the flashing.

Another was dark, and had a radio playing loudly. Then there had been a van which he had mistaken at first for an ambulance. But it had not stopped either.

– What colour was the van?

– Off-white. Grey. Maybe just a dirty white.

Then there was a people carrier with dark windows.

That was it.

– OK, said Hawthorn. He looked at Child.

– The jumper, said Child. You were wearing the jumper?

– Yes. I usually drive with my jumper on and hang my suit jacket in the back. It's more comfortable.

– What colour is it?

– The jumper? It's taupe.

Child nodded. Hawthorn had to look down at his notebook. He wrote *tawp*, and threw an important looking circle around it.

– Did you drive yourself here from the scene?

– Yes. With a police officer. She came with me.

– Your car is parked out the back?

– Yes.

– What colour is it?

Jetters looked between the two of them suspiciously.

– It's . . . blue.

– What kind of blue?

– Marine.

Child nodded, grinning. Hawthorn wrote it down.

Hawthorn called Frank Lenton.

No vintage cars could be seen on the CCTV footage they'd so far got their hands on from around Hampley Road. They were starting to examine film from earlier and later and further away. Nothing that could pass for vintage. Nothing older than an early 1990s Toyota.

Hawthorn gave Frank the possible car turning north on to Plume Road, and the rumbling engine. And he gave him the other cars and the off-white van.

Daniel Field was twenty-four, Frank told him. He lived in a house on Nestor Lane, a couple of streets away from Hampley Road, which he shared with a book editor and a post-graduate student at UCL. His parents were divorced. His father lived in Chicago, his mother in Cambridgeshire. Daniel worked in the IT department of a small French investment bank with an office near Liverpool Street. He had been due in early that morning – at 6 a.m. – for a pre-trading software update, something that happened irregularly every couple of months or so. He was gay and single. He had one younger sister who was a student in Reading. His sister and his mother were on their way to London. He had no criminal record. He had no arrest record. He did not appear on any intelligence watch list or database. He was a civilian.

Hawthorn called the hospital. Daniel Field was still in

surgery, but Hawthorn got hold of one of the nurses. Daniel would be fine. He had been hit once, in the right abdomen, the bullet ricocheting slightly off the top of his hip bone, and coming to rest close to his bladder. But it was a small bullet and had not left much damage in its wake. Surgery would take a while because they wanted it to be as unobtrusive as possible. He was generally healthy. He would make a full recovery.

Child had disappeared. Hawthorn dozed in the stuffy duty lounge of Highbury Station. He stretched out on an odd-smelling sofa with his hands on his stomach and his head turned towards the muted television. He was thinking about his father. There was a chat show on the screen, and everyone was smiling. He was not thinking anything specific about his father. He simply had him in mind. His face and voice and the grip of his hands and his smell and his eyes. His voice.

He could call him, he thought. And ask him about old cars. He remembered toys. Old toys. He remembered the carpet in the hallway, and the kitchen floor. He remembered lying down flat, with old toy cars in his hands.

He fell asleep.

He dreamed he was asleep in front of the television.

– We're getting some progress from a couple of sources in Tottenham. Pointing to a random pair of fun-gunners associated with a dealership, gone a little haywire.

Hawthorn frowned. Rivers sounded upbeat. The case was elsewhere. The case was always elsewhere. Nevertheless, he frowned, and noticed that Child picked up on it and mirrored it, and took off his glasses and rubbed his eyes.

– In a vintage car?

– Yeah. A blue Hyundai Coupe. About two years old. Does he wear glasses?

– No. At least . . .

– Find out if he wears contacts. Maybe he's partial to a pre-work spliff. Did you ask the hospital what they'd pumped into him by the time he started talking to you?

– Nothing hallucinogenic. I don't know.

– I had an assault victim once who insisted that it was the Archbishop of Canterbury in full regalia who'd jumped her on a back street in Lambeth. You'll have to wait for him to come round. Assuming he comes round. Shock. Confusion. Drifting in and out of consciousness. Maybe he didn't see it at all and the brain has filled in for him. Who knows? Don't worry about it.

– I think he was pretty sure.

– Go and speak to the housemates. They've given statements. But I want to know if any of them have any links to this Tottenham crew. It's unlikely but you never know. Do they smoke a bit? A little coke for a party sometimes? Who do they get it from? Any trouble with them? Go gently, please. My money is on random.

– OK.

25

– And stay linked to the hospital. We'll need better than a vintage car from him.

He hung up.

– We are not at the centre of things, said Child.

Hampley Road was taped off from the crossroads down to the first junction, from where Jetters had come. Hawthorn closed his eyes. The sky was grey and flat and he liked it. There was a patch of black blood on the cold path. He opened his eyes. There was a patch of blood. But it was not quite black, and it was smaller and it was in a different place. People in baby-blue paper jumpsuits and white shoe-covers were wandering around with bags and brushes and pads and cameras.

– My place was about two streets away, said Child.

– Which way?

– The other way. Other side of Plume Road.

– It's not exactly murder mile is it?

– No. It's not.

– Is Amy still here?

– No. We sold the flat, remember?

– Where did she move to?

He didn't answer.

Hawthorn faced the junction with Plume Road. He tried to picture Daniel Field on the footpath.

– It must be someone very close.

– What?

– If it's not on CCTV then it's in a garage somewhere.

– Oh fuck off.

– What?

– He didn't actually see a vintage car.

– Yes he did.

– A vintage car. With running boards?

– It's what he saw. It's what he said to Jetters. Before he had any painkillers or whatever they were giving him.

– He didn't say vintage to Jetters.

– He said *old*. He was looking for the word. As soon as you said *vintage* to him he agreed.

– He was bleeding to death. He was probably seeing his own funeral cortège.

Hawthorn looked at the silver shutters set into the side of the building that faced on to Plume Road. Just to their left was a little yellow flag affixed to the brick where the bullet had struck.

– What's in there? The shutters, I mean.

– Nothing.

– Nothing?

– It was a bakery. They used to have tiered wedding cakes in the window. Edible bride, edible groom.

– Was.

– Then it was a coffee shop. Now it's nothing. Hasn't been anything for about a year.

– Why would he say *old car*? For him to say *old car* . . . it means that *old* was the most obvious thing about it. Not a colour or a make or a shape or anything. *Old*. Old car.

— Maybe he said ochre.

They wandered along the road. A uniform tried to lift the tape for them. It snapped. Child laughed. There were a couple of hobby bobbies with clipboards waiting for passers-by. A car drove up Almond Road. They watched it. It was the way Jetters had come. Residential, quiet, speed bumps. It was a short cut, avoiding the junction at the top of Plume Road if you were coming from the north or north-east. Hawthorn wondered why Jetters felt the need for short cuts at that hour of the morning. One of the hobby bobbies stopped the car. Child walked a little down the road, on the right-hand side. He turned and walked back again slowly, looking to his right. He was trying to see what Jetters had seen. Hawthorn watched him, and looked at the walls of the houses, at the brick of the gables, at the paths. There was the ghost of some graffiti on the wall to his left, at the corner of the two roads. It had been painted over, or washed out, but a shape persisted, snaky, coming out of the side and weaving its way diagonally towards the ground. It came to the footpath where a tuft of weed climbed out of a crack. Hawthorn touched the weed with his shoe. There was a cigarette butt in there. A cigarette butt and a hair clip. Slightly to the left there was a tube ticket. A match. Two matches. There was a blacked-out smudge of old chewing gum. A little further away was a glob of pearly-green phlegm and spittle. He looked down to his feet, at the small, impossibly detailed space he occupied. His patch.

Child was back at his shoulder. They looked further up

Hampley Road. In the distance they could see officers going door to door. They'd have to do that again in the evening, when people were home. The stopped car moved off again. It turned left into Hampley Road and hesitated for a moment, working out a way around the blockage. Hawthorn let Child get ahead of him and pretended to be looking at his notebook. He found a handkerchief in his back pocket and blew his nose and pressed it to his eyes and clenched them closed and cursed until he could continue.

Nestor Lane was a short terrace that faced another in the cold, with a line of cars parked on one side. It was very quiet. The houses were pre-war, three-storey, brick, fronted by tiny gardens. Most of the gardens had been paved over one way or another and were taken up now with wheelie bins, covered motorbikes, the occasional flowerbed or small tree. Above the ground floor windows a plain stone lintel ran through the brickwork, all the way down the terrace. Next door to Daniel Field's house, at what looked like the middle of the row, there was a date elegantly etched or carved – a year – the digits separated by tiny diamond shapes. Hawthorn wrote it in his notebook.

Child had gone ahead of him and was in the kitchen. A young woman stood at the sink, and a woman police officer sat at the table with a cup of something. She nodded at Hawthorn. The woman at the sink was talking. She had been talking all the time.

– And the kids, the kids sometimes come down the road in packs, little gangs, looking for trouble, making noise. Sometimes they'll kick a football around for a while or that kind of thing, and God help you if you shout at them to get lost. I made that mistake once. Your life is a misery then. They broke a window. Everyone knows not to shout at them, and they just get bored and go away. It's the older, quieter . . . oh hello, are you another detective? I think you're the sixth now, are you? I've lost track. We haven't had this many people in the house for I don't know how long.

She was in a dressing gown. She was washing cups.

– I'm Detective Hawthorn. You must be Ms Gayle?

– Alison, yes.

She shook his hand, leaving it wet.

– Are you the boss then?

– Not as such, no. Detective Chief Inspector Rivers is leading the investigation.

– Oh yes, someone said. Tea or coffee? I don't really know what a boss is in the police. No one looks very much like a detective to me. You're all too well dressed, too young. I don't know what I'm expecting. Helen Mirren I suppose, being rude to me. No one's even been rude to me. I am sorry, I'm babbling. I tend to babble. When things are . . . is there any word?

– About Daniel? He's . . . he's still in surgery as far as I know. But I spoke to one of the nurses a while ago. And . . . unofficially as it were, he's doing well. It's going well.

– Oh thank God.

She slumped a little, closed her eyes for a moment.

– I'm sure, said Child, that you've been through all this at least a couple of times already. But if you don't mind. When was the last time you saw Daniel?

– Last night. In here. He wasn't looking forward to getting up early. He likes his sleep. He didn't know whether it was better to force himself to go to bed early or not. He was afraid he wouldn't sleep.

– Apart from that he was in a good mood?

– Yes, he was fine. He's always fine. He's very . . . he doesn't really do moods.

– You didn't hear him leave this morning?

– No. He's quiet in the mornings. He has his own floor, more or less. The top floor. Sometimes I hear him clumping around, but not this morning.

Her eyes had lost focus. She was calmer.

– Is Mr Andone still here? Hawthorn asked.

– He went to take a shower.

– Did you have a normal weekend? Child asked.

– Me? Yes.

– What about Daniel? Do you know if he was doing anything unusual this weekend?

– Not that I know of. I don't know. He was out late on Saturday. He slept late yesterday. But that's not unusual is it?

– Did he have anyone to stay?

– Not that I saw.

– Would you, typically, see people that Daniel had over?

– Sometimes, probably. On a weekend, yes, usually.

– Does he have a lot of people to stay?

She shrugged and smiled.

– What's a lot? More than I do, that's for sure.

– Anyone regular?

– Not lately, no.

– We're not investigating anything other than Daniel's shooting, but I need to ask you whether Daniel uses any drugs.

– How is that relevant?

She looked at Child, but she didn't seem particularly surprised.

– Well it may not be. But most violent crime in this city is drug related.

She thought for a moment.

– He smokes the occasional joint. That's all I know about. I'm sure that's all he does.

– Where does he get it?

She hesitated, glanced at the door.

– Walter usually has some. He gets a little extra sometimes and Dan and I will have some.

– Does he get it locally?

– No, at uni I think. He knows someone. We haven't had any in ages. Well, I haven't. And I don't think Dan has either.

Hawthorn cleared his throat.

– Do you know anyone who drives a vintage car?

Child looked at him.

– No.

– Anyone who has an old car, or an unusual one? A kit car or anything?

– I don't know what a kit car is. I don't know anyone who has any kind of car. Except our neighbours. Some people at work I suppose. I don't really know anything about cars. Why?

He didn't feel able to tell her. He wasn't sure why. He shrugged.

– It's not important, said Child. Do you pay Walter for the extra that he gets?

– Yes. Or Dan does, usually. It's not very much. A fiver here and there.

– Would you mind, Hawthorn interrupted, if I had a look around?

– Go ahead.

Child closed his eyes briefly, gave a low sigh. Hawthorn smiled at Alison Gayle.

It was a warm, well-kept house. There were wooden floors, good rugs, framed prints on the walls. But there were pieces of old, solid furniture as well. The heavy, dark kitchen table. A dresser in the hallway. Bookcases in the living room that looked made for the space.

He stood in front of them. There was a large television and a games console. In the bookcases, as well as books, there were two shelves full of DVDs and some games. On

33

one shelf there were a lot of old black-and-white films – Ealing comedies, World War II movies, lots of Hitchcock. On the other, science fiction, including TV box sets of American shows that Hawthorn recognized. The games meant nothing to him.

There were three doors off the first floor landing. The bathroom door was open and a warm mist hung in its bright light. Hawthorn paused. He could hear a radio, he thought, behind one of the closed doors. He continued up the stairs. The top floor landing was slightly smaller than the one below it. Three doors again. Hawthorn opened them.

One was a cupboard with water tanks and wooden shelving and piles of towels and bedding. The other was a small bathroom. No bath, just a shower unit, sink and toilet. It looked recently installed. There was a small stack of magazines on the window sill. Everything was clean.

The bedroom was dark, the curtains drawn. He stood in the doorway and flicked the light switch and stepped in. He closed his eyes, briefly. He inhaled. He reached out and switched the light off again. Then he switched it on. He reached for his notebook.

The bed was unmade. A duvet was piled up at its centre as if picked up and thrown there. There was a large wicker laundry basket by the door, beside a wardrobe. There was a desk to the left of the bed. There were some cables sitting on it, for his laptop presumably. There was a hard drive. There was a phone charger. Hawthorn ducked and saw a large plugboard under the table, switched off at the socket, which was to the right, under the window. There was a bedside table – a little two-drawer locker – with a lamp, a clock radio and a glass of water sitting on it. On the other side of the bed there was a chest of drawers. A couple of jumpers sat neatly folded on top. There was a pair of jeans on the floor. There was a bookcase. It was full, mostly with books, though there were also some DVDs and CDs. There were two framed prints on the wall above the desk. One was an art deco poster advertising the tube. The other was a poster for a film, or perhaps a comic book, in French.

Hawthorn switched off the light again. The curtains were heavy. They excluded most of the day. The alarm clock had green digits. There was something glinting in the corner. He switched the light on. It was a tin on the lowest of the bookshelves. A metal box. A tin. A container. Little things were perched in front of the books all over the bookshelves. Little toy-like things. A ring. An old lighter. A London snow globe. There was an iPod box, a camera, a pair of gloves. There were a couple of photographs in frames. Some postcards.

Hawthorn went over and looked at the photographs. He assumed the mother, the sister. There was a family portrait a few years old. A younger Daniel, his hair longer, his mother and sister, a man with sunglasses, his arms folded. There were two postcards. One was signed *Dad*. It showed an old-fashioned space rocket standing upright against a blue sky. It was from the NASA Space Centre in Houston. Hawthorn couldn't read the writing on the other one. It showed a view of Prague.

He walked to the door and looked out. He listened. He walked over to the stairs and looked down and listened. He could still hear the low sound of the radio on the floor below. Nothing else. He went back to the doorway of the bedroom. He turned the light off again.

He didn't move at all for a while. Then he walked quickly into the room, slipping off his jacket and kicking off his shoes. He took the duvet and spread it out properly. He looked at the door for a moment, and then he lifted the corner of the duvet and climbed into the bed.

He stared at the ceiling. The room was cold. He sniffed. He moved his legs. Then he shifted on to his left side, facing the bookcase. His left arm came out and draped itself across the pillows. He stayed like that for a couple of minutes, sniffing. Then he turned on to his right side, facing the little bedside table. He lay still for a while. Then he propped himself up on his elbow and turned on the bedside lamp.

The top drawer was full of socks and underwear. He rummaged a little and came up with two cufflink boxes, a tiepin and a pair of cheap flip-flops. In the lower drawer there were condoms, a bottle of poppers, various . . .

He heard a noise.

He switched off the lamp. Closed the drawer.

Nothing happened. He couldn't hear it now.

Then he heard a creak, like a floorboard. A door closed. Below him somewhere. There was a small silence, and then the sound of someone trotting down the stairs. Or up the stairs. Up the stairs.

He lay back on the bed. He slid down so that his head was off the pillow, flat on the mattress. A figure appeared in the doorway. It seemed to pause. To look into the room. Hawthorn could see a silhouette only, and only the upper part of that. It looked like a little old man, hunched over, regarding him, tilting his head, considering Hawthorn. Sniffing. It sniffed. It seemed to stay still for a long time. Hawthorn did not breathe. He did not move his eyes. The silhouette reached out towards him. It seemed to. Then it was gone. There was the click of the airing-cupboard door opening. And a silence. Then the same click again. Closing. There were human noises – a half cough, a throat clearing, another sniff. Then feet, trotting down the stairs.

He got out of the bed and put on his shoes and his jacket and turned on the light and wrote down some of the book titles. There was a lot of history. He looked in the tin box, the container that had glinted in the dark. He struggled with the lid. It was empty.

– I'm not interested in anything other than the shooting. I'm not investigating Daniel.

– It sounds like you are.

– Really, I'm not.

– Walter, just tell him.

– It has nothing to do with anything.

– It probably doesn't. But I'm sure you'd want to be certain. For peace of mind. I'm not interested in some minor pot buying, believe me. Or selling.

– I know . . .

Hawthorn stepped into the kitchen.

– Who are you?

Walter Andone was small, muscular, clean-shaven, dark-haired. His accent was very lightly East European, or possibly Italian.

– I'm Detective Hawthorn.

– May I see some ID please?

– Oh, Walter, for Christ's sake.

– Of course.

Hawthorn rummaged for it, smiling. Alison Gayle looked apologetically at him.

– Did you find your way around all right? she asked.

– Thanks, yes.

– You were upstairs?

Hawthorn glanced at Child and Alison Gayle. He found his warrant card and held it out.

– Yes. You must be Mr Andone.

He snatched the card from Hawthorn's hand.

– Where were you? Doing what?

Hawthorn smiled at him.

– I was having a look in Daniel's room.

Andone stared at him. Not at the card. He hadn't even looked at the card.

– Just now?

– Yes. I was in the living room as well. That's all. Who's the movie buff?

Andone continued to stare.

– You have a search warrant?

– No.

– I thought you needed a warrant to search anywhere.

– It's not a search, said Child. But in any case, when someone is the victim of a crime, the law allows us to assume consent in relation to their premises.

Child spoke genially. Andone nodded, his eyes on Hawthorn. He looked at the card and handed it back.

– What are you looking for?

– We're just trying to get an idea of who might have wanted to shoot Daniel.

It was Child who was talking, but Andone looked at Hawthorn.

– In his room?

– We don't have the benefit of knowing him. How long have you known him?

– A year. A little more.

Hawthorn said nothing.

– I am not telling you anything about any drugs. I am saying nothing about it whatsoever.

Child sighed.

– Well tell me this at least. Do you know any dealers who are local?

Andone turned his attention to Child.

– No. I can say that. No.

– Do you know any from Tottenham?

He considered this. Hawthorn stood by the wall.

– No. Not at all.

– Do you know, Hawthorn said, anyone who owns a vintage car?

Andone glared at him again.

– A vintage car? No.

– Tottenham, said Child. Do you have any connection with Tottenham? With anyone in Tottenham who is involved in selling drugs?

– From a vintage car?

– Forget the vintage car.

– No. I do not know anyone from Tottenham.

They all looked at each other. Hawthorn took out his notebook. The others watched him do that, as if they expected something to come of it.

Child coughed.

– OK, he said. OK. If you do think of any connection to Tottenham, please let us know. It could be very important.

As they walked back to the car Hawthorn looked through his notebook while Child talked. While Child complained. *Hunched . . . tin box . . . NASA.* He complained about Andone and Alison Gayle. *Marine . . . pools of light/pools of shadow*

. . . *ribbing.* He complained about Hawthorn. *London, A Biography . . . Jewish London . . . The Man Who Knew Too Much.* He complained about the car.

Hawthorn read his notebook while he pretended to listen to Child. Or, he listened to Child while he pretended to read his notebook. He didn't know which it was.

Daniel Field was alive and would recover. He was heavily sedated and sleeping. A family liaison officer met them outside an intensive care waiting room. Through the small window in the door they could see Mrs Field pacing up and down, talking on the telephone while her daughter sat in a corner, her attention fixed on the mobile phone in her hand. They waited.

– Did he regain consciousness at all? Hawthorn asked.

– Briefly, yes, in recovery.

– And?

– And what?

– What did he say?

– Nothing. After four hours of surgery? Nothing at all.

– Who's she talking to?

– Her ex-husband. Any arrests yet?

– Last seen heading north, said Child. They think they're in Manchester. There's pictures of them all the way up the M6.

– In the Hyundai?

– In the Hyundai. Not the brightest, these boys.

– And crack high.

– This is the third of these in the last year.

– Third?

– One down in Peckham last summer. And the guy in Vauxhall.

– Vauxhall was a hit.

– Was it?

Hawthorn watched Mrs Field. She was about five foot eight tall in her heels, late forties, attractive, her grey hair cut short. She was dressed in a black business suit. She glanced up and caught his eye. He looked away.

She kept them waiting some time. When she came to the door she looked them over. She said nothing, and allowed Hawthorn then Child to introduce themselves. They went into the room. She introduced her daughter. Her face was marked by tears and she seemed very young. Mrs Field asked where Rivers was. Child told her about the boys from Tottenham and the trail that was being followed northwards. She nodded, rubbed at her eyes.

– Random is never really random, she said quietly.

– What do you mean? Hawthorn asked.

She looked up at him, a little surprised, and then she almost smiled.

– I don't mean that it wasn't random. I just mean that it doesn't feel random when it happens to your son. It feels very specific then. Very specific.

– When we spoke to Daniel this morning . . . Hawthorn began.

– You spoke to him?

– Yes. We got here just as he did. We were able to speak to him very briefly in the emergency room.

– Oh. I didn't know. How was . . . I mean . . . was he in pain? Hawthorn lifted his shoulders a little.

– Well yes, he was in pain. Of course he was in pain.

– They were preparing him for surgery, said Child. He was given painkillers very quickly. They were looking after him very well.

– I know. Of course. It's just difficult for me to think about. Was he very frightened?

– He was actually quite alert, said Hawthorn. He seemed strong. It was a good sign. They said it was a good sign.

She pushed a smile towards her daughter. Nodded.

– When we spoke to him, Hawthorn went on, we asked him what had happened. He told us that a car had pulled up alongside him and shots had been fired. But he told us that it was an old car. An old-fashioned car. And when we asked did he mean a vintage car he said yes. A vintage car.

She frowned.

– But these boys . . . were they in a vintage car?

– No.

– The simple explanation, said Child, is that Daniel, in shock, perhaps coming under the influence of the first of the painkillers and what have you, imagined that he had seen a vintage car.

– Yes, she said quietly.

– But it's a loose end, said Child. And my colleague is keen to tie it up.

– Do you know anyone with a vintage car? Have you heard Daniel mention knowing anyone with a vintage car?

She was quiet. She didn't move. Then she shook her head slowly.

– Does a vintage car mean anything to you at all?

– No. Not really.

– Not really?

– Not at all. That I can think of.

– There are no . . . you don't know anyone who drives, who owns, a vintage car?

She appeared to think about it for a moment.

– No.

Hawthorn nodded.

– Does Daniel own the house on Nestor Lane?

– Yes. He does. He inherited it from his grandfather. His father's father.

– How long has it been in the family?

– I really don't know. 1930s I think.

Daniel Field lay flat on his bed. His torso below the chest was bound in bandages. Various lines and tubes and cables came and went from his arms, and under the covers which lay on his lower body. There was dark bruising on his left shoulder. His face seemed slightly swollen. There was a scratch on his left cheek that Hawthorn didn't remember from the morning.

Mrs Field and her daughter had already spent twenty minutes with him before the daughter came out and told Hawthorn and Child to come in.

– Did he tell you anything about the shooting?

– Just what you said. An old car. Then Mum got him to stop and sent me to get you.

He was pale. Dull blue veins were scribbled across his skin. His hands were clean.

His mother touched his arm above his wrist. He opened his eyes. It seemed to take a moment for him to focus on her. She kissed his forehead.

– Go on, Daniel.

– What?

– Tell us what you remember.

He looked confused for a moment, and he looked around her, into the gloom. He looked at Child and Hawthorn, and his sister, then back at Hawthorn.

– Oh, he said. Yeah.

He closed his eyes, and Hawthorn thought that he'd drifted off. But his mother stroked his arm, and after a moment he started to speak softly.

– There was . . . a black car. Low down. With those running boards. And those old silver door handles. Like in a black-and-white film. The window was down. I couldn't see anyone. Just a flash. I don't remember a bang. A flash, and I didn't know . . . nothing happened. I thought it was a camera flash. I thought someone was taking my picture. The car was lovely.

Silent, low down. Sweeping. Then there was another . . . flash and . . . boof . . . I felt like I'd been . . . punched in the stomach. Then I was on the ground, and the pain came, and I felt like something really bad had happened in my stomach, or somewhere. Inside me. Something had exploded. But I heard no noise. No bang . . . nothing. Like the sound was down. I thought someone was taking my photograph while my insides were exploding, and I hoped they'd call an ambulance, but then they were gone and my hand was covered in blood, and I realized that I'd been shot. By the car.

He opened his eyes briefly and looked at Hawthorn, as if to check that he was still there. Then he closed them again.

– I thought it was the stupidest thing that could ever have happened.

Child shrugged in the corridors.

– You're not happy, are you? he said.

– He saw what he saw.

– He saw what he thought he saw.

– He's been completely consistent.

– And vague. A low dark car. With running boards. A lovely car.

– Silver door handles.

– Silver door handles.

– It's no more vague than descriptions we get from people who don't know cars. We explicate.

– We what?

– Explicate?

– I don't think that's the right word, Hawthorn.

– We put them together.

– Extrapolate?

– Yeah.

– We work it out. But. You know. I'm not sure we have a model book that goes back to . . . whenever. If he insists on it the CPS will have a bit of a problem.

They wandered through the corridors. Hawthorn assumed Child knew where he was going.

– What it is, said Child, is that you don't want to go back to Mishazzo.

Hawthorn looked at him.

– What?

– It's a hallucination, or whatever. Rivers has it tied up. You want a loose thread so that we're not back following that idiot all day long. Looking at windows. Going slowly insane.

– It's not that.

– And Rivers is being a prick. I know that. It wasn't our fault we lost the driver. So I get it. Really. If there was anything believable about it I'd go along. But what do we do with a vague description of some sort of vintage car, when we've got CCTV of the Hyundai, and two crack-high idiots weaving their way north? I wouldn't put it past them to have just thrown the gun on the back seat.

– Still. We can't just decide things that don't fit are hallucinations.

– No. We usually don't decide anything about things that don't fit. They just don't fit. So we leave them out. Least with this there's an explanation why it doesn't fit.

He hunched his shoulders and took a turn without looking. Hawthorn glanced at a sign board. He saw nothing about an exit.

– It's like Jetters, Child said. He thought he heard *ochre*. We know he didn't. But he was convinced that's what he heard. So, should we start looking for an ochre-coloured car?

Hawthorn was hating this conversation now.

– It's different.

– No it's not. It's people imagining things. We start investigating what people imagine . . .

He trailed off, looked over his shoulder.

– Where the fuck are we?

Hawthorn shook his head. They turned another corner.

– It's not even plausible, Child went on. The vintage car. You know there was a camera pointing all the way up Plume Road? From down near the tube. Looking all the way back up. You can see the junction with Hampley Road. It's in the distance, but you can see it. This is a traffic camera so it's digital whatever. It has the timer on it, and it's clear. And at exactly the right time, the Hyundai comes around that corner. Nothing before. Nothing after. No vintage cars. Just the Hyundai. And no vintage cars.

Hawthorn looked at him. He hated it.

– You know what those things are like.

Child laughed.

– No, I know what they're like when they don't fit. I know how suddenly when it's the wrong thing on the camera the timer mysteriously gets scrambled, or a bird shits on the lens, or somebody deletes the wrong file. But this is straightforward. It's simple. There are no other explanations.

Hawthorn looked at him.

– There are several other explanations.

– Such as?

– There are dozens.

They were near the café. They paused at the junction of three corridors and looked around.

– Name one.

– There are hundreds.

Hawthorn took the turning to the left, towards a flickering light.

– Do you know where we are? Child asked him.

– No, he said. There are millions of explanations. There's an infinite number of explanations.

Child sighed and pushed his glasses up the ramp of his nose.

– Well you can do the paperwork then.

Hawthorn went online. He looked up film titles, book titles. He tried to discover the history of the house on Nestor Lane, and of Nestor Lane itself. He looked at cars. At pictures of cars. He found some that seemed about right. He printed off the photographs of seven of them. He tried to put all the photographs on one page but couldn't work the software.

Child had gone home. Two men had been arrested in Bolton and were on their way back to London. No sign of the gun. They denied everything. They knew nothing about any shooting, they said. But Rivers had put them in separate vans with someone to talk to.

Hawthorn asked Frank Lenton to show him the CCTV footage. Plume Road looked long; a strip of grey with white highlights and black shadows. It was still as a photograph. He watched the wrong junction the first time. Frank replayed it. A speck of something half bright crawled around the corner from Hampley Road. It looked low down to Hawthorn.

– That's it?

The car hesitated and then turned north, away from the camera, its rear lights like pinprick stars that faded as soon as he looked at them. He wasn't sure that they weren't just reflections.

– Yeah. They can zoom in on it.

– Can you?

– No. I don't have the gear.

They watched it a few times. Hawthorn squinted. He tried looking slightly to the side, to catch it out of the corner of his eye. He tried to stare at it directly. He tried to pretend he didn't know it was coming. But every time he saw it, it looked like nothing. It was formless. He could imagine it into any shape he thought of. He could make it disappear by imagining that it wasn't there at all – that he didn't see it. The road was empty and was not a road. He found himself looking at the smudged screen.

– Thank you, Frank.

The city fell apart into silence and darkness and cold, and Hawthorn took a bus to Finsbury Park and then walked up to Crouch End and ate pasta in the Italian place by the green. It was quiet. He tried to take his time. He tried to wait before each mouthful. He couldn't decide what to think about.

He called his brother. They talked about the weekend. They talked about their father. They talked about Tess's new computer. Hawthorn asked his brother what he knew about vintage cars.

– What kind of vintage?

– Pre-war. 1930s I think.

– What about them?

– Do you see many?

– Nah, I don't think so. If there's an event maybe. The London to Brighton, you see them then. There's a restored nineteen forty something cab I see around. I don't know the cabbie. I used to have a regular fare from Chelsea to Ealing, was a vintage car dealer I think. Driving ban. Why?

– Ealing?

– Yeah. Ealing. Why?

– Case.

– Theft?

– No, not really. I'll tell you about it at the weekend.

– You all right?

– Yeah, I'm fine.

He was on his second coffee. They were starting to close up.

– How's the thing?

– What thing?

– The crying.

Hawthorn made a face and looked out of the window.

– It's fine. Do you remember the models? Dad's models? Soldiers and cars and that?

– Yeah, I do. I remember the soldiers. Lead things. Painted. They were Granddad's, I think. Haven't seen them in years.

– There used to be cars too. Heavy. Solid. Were they lead?

– Lead paint. Cast iron. Probably be worth something now. Did you not get into trouble about them?

– Yeah. I broke a few. I used to crash them together. Chipped them. Knocked wheels off and that.

– Violent little tyke, you were. You get a thrashing?

– No, I got a talk.

– Ah. A talk.

– I still remember it. Made me feel like a bastard.

– Which you were.

– Which I was.

– We should ask him about them. You going to come over on Saturday?

– Yeah, that's the plan.

– All right. Tess says love, and the kids.

– Love back.

In the roads on the hill he looked at the city lights and the airplanes circling over south London like a lid closing on a jar. He stamped to keep his feet warm and tried to get lost. He took a bus to Muswell Hill and took a bus back again. He had another coffee in a tiny Turkish place and pretended to talk about football. He sent text messages that were vague. He thought about various people. He sat on a bench in Highgate with a view over everything and let himself cry a little. It wasn't so bad. It stopped after about ten minutes. He wondered why he didn't want to go home. It was not far. He could go home and have a shower.

He kept walking. He drank more coffee in an all-night McDonald's. He dozed off for a while. By the time the staff woke him up he was almost late. He started walking back towards Finsbury Park.

He stood outside the house on Nestor Lane. There was silence. The night was dark and the street lamps were like hoods. He looked up at the windows. He expected to see Walter Andone looking back at him, his face against the glass. Then he expected to see Walter Andone's silhouette. Reaching out to him. The windows were all curtained. The upstairs ones seemed frosted with condensation. The date sat in the corner of his eye, on the right, like a time stamp in a photograph. The house did not look that old. It did not look like shelter. It did not look like a place where you might go to be warm, to sleep, to sit with loved ones and retreat from the day and from the city. It looked like something you would grit your teeth to enter. It looked like all the city surrounded it as an ante-chamber, a place to rest, and it was the building that contained all the work and the toil and the pain of things.

He walked. He walked with his hands in his pockets. He pretended that there was nothing in his mind.

Things come out of the past.

They had taken down the tape on Hampley Road and it was open to traffic. There was no traffic. There were incident boards. *Shooting. Witnesses. Serious injury. Please call.* He look-ed up towards Plume Road and paused. Cars in the distance sounded like other things, natural things. Waves on water. The wind in leaves. He walked along the path and listened to his footsteps.

He came to Daniel Field's blood, dried on the path like old chewing gum. There was a discarded swab stick in the gutter. At the foot of the wall lay the yellow marker, fallen from the place where the stray bullet had struck. He stared at the silver shutter. It was dull in the gloom. It was cold. He looked at his watch and retraced his steps a little. Then he pretended he was Daniel Field and walked as if on his way to the tube station. He imagined he was carrying a shoulder bag. His head natu-rally turned towards the ground. He looked at the little bit of London at his feet, at the smudges and marks, the scuffs and scratches, the tiny scraps of paper stuck to the stone. Tiredness allowed everything to flow into everything else. There was nothing distinct. A head full of condensation. He moved over the black marks of dropped liquids, cigarettes, spit, blood, dog shit, pollen and rain. In a thousand years this would all be buried. He halted at the stain. He heard a car come up behind him.

He didn't turn. He looked ahead. The car edged into his field of vision, slowly and smoothly, its wheels turning in the corner of his eye like a thought. It was dark. A dark car. But it was not black. There were no running boards. There were no silver handles.

– Detective. Hello there. Detective?

Hawthorn turned. He looked back up Hampley Road. It was empty. He looked towards Plume Road. Then he looked down at the car in front of him. He had to drop to his haunches to talk to the driver.

– Hello, Mr Jetters.

– How is he? Daniel, I mean.

– He's good. He'll be fine. He's expected to make a full recovery.

Jetters turned briefly and looked ahead. He smiled.

– That is great. That is great to hear.

– His mother, said Hawthorn. She asked if she could contact you. Do you mind if I give her your details?

– No, no. Not at all. I'd quite like to visit him I think.

Hawthorn nodded.

– And have you caught anyone?

– Arrests have been made. Can't say too much about that.

– Of course. Well. That's all very good news.

– Yeah. Yeah it is.

– What has you out here then?

Hawthorn shrugged.

– It would be good to have another witness. Someone who might walk this way in the mornings. That kind of thing.

Jetters nodded. He wished Hawthorn luck. He drove to Plume Road and turned left.

Hawthorn stood at the corner of Hampley Road and Plume Road, beside one of the incident boards. It was five minutes or more before anyone appeared. He showed his ID card. Then he showed the pictures. The pictures of the cars.

– Have you seen anything like this? Perhaps not exactly. But something like this. Or this one? Does that mean anything to you?

People shook their heads. Squinted. Took the pages from his hand and held them up to the light. People took out their reading glasses. They thought about it. They wanted to help. But none of them had seen anything like that.

– Or any sort of vintage car. Old car. 1930s probably. Like in the movies.

He stayed there an hour. It was cold. He was tired. He could not think. He lost count of the number of people he stopped. He wasn't sure. Afterwards he thought he had possibly been crying. With some of them. Not all of them.

Some of them. Then he realized that it was getting busier and that there were too many – too many people. He was missing most of them, and he thought that he might look like he was crying. Because he was so tired. And no. No one had seen anything like that. And they'd remember, they said. They'd remember something like that.

He went home. He wept in his bed, out of tiredness, he thought. Merely tiredness. That was fine. He fell asleep.

He dreamed that he slept in a house that moved, and that was not his, and that was not now.

Goo Book

It was fucking hot.

He could feel something on his thigh, a bruise. It felt like a bruise, sweet and small, and he poked it with his finger a couple of times. He didn't know how he'd got that. He rolled it around his body like a taste.

Sometimes he found cuts where he thought he was only bruised.

Car fumes grimed his skin. He moved through the arches with his shirt hanging from his back pocket and a pair of stall sunglasses biting his nose, the pads missing. He weaved around the pillars and the statues and he stopped by the drinking fountain and watched for a while, but there were only schoolkids and builders and one or two guys like him. Tourists never drank from the drinking fountain.

He had left her by the canal, dozing on the grass in the shade with his tobacco and his weed and his lighter and his keys and his wallet, and she was probably snoring now, dreaming. Or she was being robbed, raped, murdered, bullied, torn apart, and if the canal had a tide she would drown, just for him, just because of him, because he had thought of it, and then he would have that instead of her.

You can love someone too much.

He scratched his armpit and poked the bruise and tried to stop thinking about her.

By the gallery doors there was a group of old Japanese or Chinese or something tourists, and they all had bags hanging off their shoulders. He slapped himself on the face a couple of times and worked up the bright smile, and put on his shirt and patted down his hair, and he slid through them like Jesus through children, smiling at them and saying *ciao ciao*, and they smiled back at him and one or two clutched their cameras and laughed, and he lowered his arms and paused for the entrance and they forgot about him and he came out the other side with a box purse and what his fingers had thought was a wallet but which turned out to be a notebook. Not very fucking good then.

He stopped around the corner where the cameras didn't reach and he looked at the notebook. It was full of writing in different coloured inks. Pages covered in strange script. There was a photograph of a small girl, taken in the black-and-white past. Shit. He went back to the corner and picked out a shy-looking schoolboy and gave him the notebook and told him to give it to one of the Japanese outside the gallery, and to do it immediately and to do it right or he'd fucking kill him, and he gave him a couple of quid. Then he took off his shirt again, counted the cash from the purse and pocketed it, and threw the purse in a bin, and the sunglasses as well.

She was sitting up, dazed, staring in to the water. He kissed her and stroked her back, but she was too hot and she shrugged him off. She picked up her things and they walked towards the road, and he hailed a taxi and they went home and she got in the shower and he gave her a few minutes, then he climbed in beside her and they stood together in the cool water and they held each other skin to skin, and he was the happiest he had ever been, again, and he had no worries, none, and he worried about that.

He stole from tourists. Everyone steals from tourists. He stole honest. He put his hand in their pockets. And he had arrange-ments with the night managers at a couple of hotels. Maybe twice a week he'd get a call. Sometimes he worked as a driver for a man called Mishazzo, but that was irregular. Mishazzo was a gentleman. He was small and thin like a teenager, so he always wore a beard and an expensive suit, and sometimes he carried an umbrella when there was no sign of rain, and he sat quietly in the back with his legs crossed, smoking or reading the paper or talking on the phone. There were other men who worked for Mishazzo. There was Price. Some younger ones. They would pile into the car without Mishazzo and direct him somewhere and then they would pile out and be gone for a while and sometimes he heard shouting.

He didn't like violence.

*

She was younger than him. They had friends; that was how they'd met. Her brother used to go out with his friend Derek's sister, when they were kids. They all went to the same two pubs and the same shitty club in Waltham Cross. Noisy friends, and their voices in the middle of all that, and their voices went quiet when they met. And their friends knew quicker than they did. Her mother said it was a bad crowd, but it wasn't.

She hated her name. He hated his name.

Price was a professional.

– I am a professional. You hear me? You need to be a professional too. You hear me? You need to show up shaved and showered and wearing a shirt. No fucking trainers. You will never show up after you've been drinking or smoking or taking whatever the fuck it is you take. Never. If I call you and need you, and you've been drinking, you fucking tell me. *I've had a couple of glasses of wine, Mr Price. I've just smoked a fat spliff, Mr Price. I'm out of my fucking mind on meth, Mr Price.* The inconvenience this will cause me is as nothing to the fucking mess I will make of you if you ever turn up anything less than stone-cold fucking sober. You hear me? Pro-fucking-fessional.

He nodded, smiling.

– You are, needless to say, completely fucking deaf, blind, mute. You are a stone. You are stupid. You understand nothing. You remember nothing. You drive the fucking car. And that is all you fucking do. You hear me?

– Yes, sir.

His father had put him in touch with Price. He didn't
know the story. His father knew a lot of people. His father
came and went. His father thought he was soft. He didn't trust
his father.

They couldn't talk. They were not good talkers, either of them.
And once, long ago now, she had bought a notebook for a
course. It lay empty and forgotten on the kitchen table until
one afternoon, when she had gone out to the shops and he
was worried that she would be killed by a bus or by lightning,
he opened the notebook and he wrote lines about how he
loved her, the way he loved her, about his fucking heart and
crap like that, about his body brimful and his scrambled head.
All that. She came back from the shops. He left the notebook
where it was, and he didn't mention it. And it wasn't until
about a week later that he noticed it again, and he flicked it
open, and he saw his lines followed by lines from her. She'd
written words that she had never said. He sat down. He read
them over and over for a long time. Then he wrote a para-
graph for her to find.

This went on for ages before either of them said anything
about it. But he thought that maybe they touched each other
differently. It was like the book freed stuff up, allowed it to
happen, that the tenderness was covered, they had it covered,
they had all the love and kindness and gentleness covered, and
the sex became something else.

*

He had never seen anyone die. He'd never seen a body.

Sometimes when it was just Price and some of the others they would get back in the car and laugh and shout and punch the back of his seat.

– Did you see his fucking face?

– Thought you were going to have his fucking arm off!

– I swear I've broken a fucking finger!

He thought that this was probably for his benefit. That they'd done nothing other than have a chat or maybe shout at someone a bit.

He drove Mishazzo to a meeting in a suburb where he had never been before, to an industrial estate that seemed abandoned, but only temporarily, as if it was the weekend, even though it was a Tuesday. He sat in the car waiting. He read a newspaper. Then there was a shot – a sound like a shot – and he looked around but he couldn't see anybody, and he wasn't sure if it had been a shot at all. What does a shot sound like? He saw Mishazzo in the rear-view mirror and he started the engine, and he saw Mishazzo hurry, and he frowned at the frown on Mishazzo's face, and as he drove off he waited for something to be said, but nothing was said. It was only when they were some distance away that Mishazzo spoke.

– Slow down.

Hours, sometimes. He sat in the car outside somewhere or other. Warehouses, electrical shops, pubs now and then. A lot of the time he had to wait around the corner, on a side street, his eyes peeled for wardens. Sometimes he just had to drive around in a circle, waiting for Mishazzo to emerge. Furniture shops, little lawyers' offices, cafés, a house in East Ham. A minicab place in Walthamstow. He would smoke with the windows open. He'd get out and lean against the door. He wasn't allowed to go anywhere. He sent texts. He started keeping an empty plastic bottle under the driver's seat. He thought of things to write in the book, and he would try to remember them until he got home. It was like trying to hold water in his hands, and sometimes he made it back and sometimes he didn't. He decided that whenever he forgot something it wasn't a loss but a correction.

He went dipping less and drove more. The money was better. Price generally told him a couple of days in advance when he'd be needed. He could calculate. He liked to have Saturdays so that he could do the matches and the tube crowds, and that was OK because Mishazzo took weekends off most of the time. The money was good. He bought her stupid little presents until she told him to stop, Jesus.

When he was naked she would look at all of him, and move him around to see what would happen, and she would keep him still and tether him. She got some straps from somewhere. Then he bought ropes, and collars. They sometimes had to stop, a little spooked, sweating and laughing suddenly, something breaking the spell. She was better at ropes. She said it was because she wasn't as self-conscious about the whole thing, that he had a sort of leftover embarrassment. And because he was used to trying to touch people so that they didn't notice. He had to practise, she said, and he'd get better.

Mishazzo asked him questions.

– Do you gossip?

– No sir. I don't gossip.

– Why not?

– I don't know.

– You don't know why you don't gossip?

– Not really.

– Are you not interested in people?

– Not really.

– What are you interested in?

– Myself, he said.

He could see Mishazzo nodding in the rear-view mirror and that was the end of the conversation.

He thought about how *myself* really meant him and her together. He could say *myself*, and mean another person as well. It didn't feel like he was leaving anything out.

They kept the book in a drawer in the kitchen. They never looked at it together. It came out of the drawer only when one of them was alone in the flat. He was afraid someone would find it. Once he moved it when her mother was coming over.

– Where the fuck is it?

– What?

– You know.

– What?

She looked at him like he was the stupidest fucking idiot she had ever seen.

– It's not in the drawer, she said.

Slow, sharp, so that he'd understand.

He smiled at her.

– It's not fucking funny. Where is it?

– It's on top of the kitchen cupboard.

She couldn't reach. She was clambering up on top of a chair when he went to get it down for her.

– Don't do that again.

– OK.

It was fucking hot.

He was mingling with a match crowd – burly men with burly wallets, hip pockets, drink taken, everyone happy and hugging. Replica shirts, T-shirts, no shirts. Home wins were the best. If they lost they were surly – mean-eyed and watchful. He picked out a pot-bellied man who was keeping a close eye on his two boys, guiding them, pointing things out, steering them away from the drunks and the shirtless thickets. One of the boys kept clutching his father's belt for a tow. He manoeuvred to the boy's side, coming towards them out of a raucous knot of beery singing, and bumped against him gently, laughing, getting the timing just about right, and veered behind his mark, whose attention was down at the bumped boy reaching for the reassuring belt. It was all good.

He stuck the wallet down his jeans and moved towards the path.

They took him from both sides, quietly, two great grips on his arms, whispering his name and that they wanted a word, no trouble now or it'd be the van. *Don't let's make a scene, son.* Or it'd be Sunday night in a cell, and the magistrate first thing Monday morning. How did they know his name? He sucked in his stomach hoping the wallet would fall into his crotch where they might not search him, or if he was lucky all the way down his leg and out on to the ground. But it stuck on his bollocks, and as they opened the car door one of them held his hand out for it. They weren't uniforms.

– What?

– The wallet.

– The what?

– Don't be a stupid fucking cunt.

They were the worst kind of police. Suits. Relaxed. Blank-faced, youngish, stone-eared. They looked like estate agents. He fished the wallet out of his jeans. They pushed him on to the back seat. One sat beside him, the other sat in the front and turned around.

It was Mishazzo they wanted. He felt stupid for not even suspecting it until they said it. He felt stupid but he kept his face still. They wanted a relationship. A friendly chat every now and again.

– I know what you're thinking. For dipping a wallet? Well, there's the hotels. There's the routine you have down in Angel, and the one you have in that boutique place in Shoreditch. We have you on camera for both of those, some nice DNA in the last room you did, with the dead-drunk guy sleeping through the whole thing.

The policeman laughed like he'd seen it.

– We have you as far back as April in Shoreditch. Nice targets. Clever stuff. I like it. Dodgy types, but wobbly. Little out of their depth. They get a couple of girls in, they snort some coke, they're not quite sure if they've been robbed sometimes. And they never want to report it even if they are. But we still have you on at least three in Angel and five in Shoreditch.

The one in the front seat was doing all the talking. His glasses reflected bits of the car. Every now and then he pushed them back up his nose. The other one sat next to him saying nothing, looking at him, at the side of his face.

– I know what you're thinking. You're thinking you'll go and see nice Mr Mishazzo and tell him all about it. I can tell you what he'll say. He'll tell you to take your chance in court with whatever we have and he'll see to it that you don't get too badly fucked up inside, and when you get out you go and see him and he'll find something for you to do. And that's you married to Mishazzo for the rest of your life. And you proposed.

He looked at the other one. His face was crooked. He looked the younger of the two, maybe. He smiled as well. It was all very civilized.

– Or, said this one, his crooked face falling straight when he talked. You could take my phone number. You could go back home and have a nice relaxed Sunday night and enjoy the rest of your week, and you could keep doing the driving, and whatever else comes up, for Mr Mishazzo. And let us know. Nothing dramatic. Just where you take him, who he meets, what he says on the phone, that kind of thing. We're not asking you to *do* anything. Just listen. And be your own man. Able to walk away from him and from us any time you like. Safe. You stop the hotels. But apart from that, nothing. You just have a couple of new friends.

They let him think about it. They never mentioned her once.

He went home and cooked for her and she sang bits of things at him and laughed at her own voice. They lay together in front of the television for a while and then she wanted him to tie her up, to practise his knots, to fuck her, come on her, fuck her again.

Mishazzo said to him:

– When you turn to the right you have a tendency to cut the corner. To slice it. Ever so slightly. When you turn left it's not a problem. You are leaning to the right. Do you have a limp?

– No.

– You're right-handed?

– Yes.

– Your legs are the same length?

– Yes.

– And your arms?

– Yes, I think so.

– You get your eyes tested?

– My eyes are fine.

– One isn't weaker than the other?

– No. My eyesight is . . . you know. Twenty twenty.

Mishazzo looked around the backseat.

– Do you dress to the right?

He laughed.

– I think it goes down the left side actually. You know. If anywhere.

In the mirror Mishazzo nodded.

– Well, that explains it then.

She worked a couple of days a week in a café in Stoke Newington. Serving, and some cooking too. Frying eggs and bacon, making sandwiches. She didn't like it when he came in. But he came in anyway, sometimes, when he was nearby.

– Let's go on a holiday, he said.

– Where?

– Anywhere.

She thought about it.

– Spain, she said.

– You've been to Spain.

– I liked it.

– You don't want to go somewhere new?

She wrapped an arm around his hip.

– I didn't see everything they have there.

– We could go to France. Or Morocco. Derek went to Morocco, said it was great.

– We could go to Spain and then get the boat to Morocco.

– How long does that take?

– It's really close. Really short.

– Is it?

– Yeah. If you look at it on a map. It's where Spain and Africa nearly touch.

At home, she went online and found a map. They looked up ferries and prices. He wondered whether they could live in Morocco. They could probably live more easily in Spain. He wondered what they could do. He could learn Spanish.

He thought that Mishazzo probably had lots of friends in Spain.

– So then now. What are you interested in?

– Sir?

Mishazzo was sitting on the back seat with his legs crossed, smoking a cigarette, looking at him in the rear-view mirror.

– Is it money? Are you interested in money?

– Yes, I am.

– Well of course. You think I pay you well?

– Yes sir.

Mishazzo was smiling. He had come out of a meeting in a Golders Green café, all smiles. Now they were stuck in traffic on the Hampstead Heath back road.

– You have a girl?

He blushed. It was the first time Mishazzo had asked. He had a plan. He had the whole thing worked out and ready. But still he blushed.

– A boy?

– No. I have a girlfriend.

– It's a serious thing? A love thing?

– No, not really. We get on well. But it's . . . it's not very serious.

– You live with her?

– We share, yes. It's more convenient that way. Financially. Makes sense.

– You love her?

– It's more like a friendship.

– You love your friends though.

– I suppose. But it's a different sort of love.

He nodded in the mirror, his face behind smoke.

They sat still for a while. Mishazzo rarely liked the radio. Sometimes he requested a CD. He liked world music. African. Middle Eastern. He would tap his hand on his knee, or bounce his leg up or down. He liked joyful music.

– I'll see. Maybe you can do more driving. And maybe some other things too. You are very young, and you have no face. So. More money for you. And your girlfriend.

When they got into Highgate Mishazzo told him to pull in to the side of the road and to turn around and look at him.

– You should be careful who you make your friend. And who you take into your bed. They are different things. If you mix them up you lose . . . perspective on both of them. Do not mix them up. That is my advice to you, my friend. The dick has no loyalty. Only the heart. But your head manages them both. So be clever. Be happy. Have fun. Have money. Have beautiful girls. Have a good life. Do not fuck your friends. Only your lovers. Never fuck your friends.

He met Hawthorn in some coffee shop on Stroud Green Road, full of people with laptops. He looked at screens and bags and people's faces. He didn't know if they were students or what. They took a table outside. It was hot. Hawthorn was wearing a T-shirt and jeans. He was less like a cop. But his leg jigged up and down all the time and his hair was cut.

– Are you off duty?

– Not really.

Hawthorn asked him where he'd been on Thursday and Friday. He got him to go through the times, the route he'd taken. How many phone calls had Mishazzo made? What had he said? What names did he use? Had he opened his briefcase? What was in it? What sort of mood was Mishazzo in? He bought the coffees. After he'd asked his questions and written some stuff down in his notebook he sat back in his chair and smiled.

– Now I'm off duty.

The way he'd said it, it sounded like a sort of come-on.

They looked at each other. Hawthorn half blushed, up near the tops of his cheeks, like some invisible thing had just flicked fingernails against his face. He looked away.

Nothing happened for a while. Then Hawthorn looked back at him. Held his eyes. For exactly the amount of time it takes for a look like that to become a look like that.

They met sometimes in the coffee shop on Stroud Green Road, sometimes in a pub in Holloway. Or near Hawthorn's flat, so that they could go there, if they wanted to. Sometimes he met Child as well, and then they usually just sat in Child's car, or they drove around. Hawthorn wrote in his notebook. He got the feeling that they knew everything already. That he was just confirming stuff. Maybe they were testing him. He made a few things up. He told them about a route he hadn't taken. Said they'd gone out to Hackney when they hadn't. Nothing seemed to surprise them. He didn't understand why any of it was important – the roads and the times – unless they were trying to trip him up. He knew the names were important. The phone calls, the buildings and houses and cafés he waited outside. The bits of conversations.

He thought that it was all probably bullshit. That he wasn't telling them anything they needed to know. They would spend six months getting him used to them, and then they would start to press. See if you can find out this or that. Or maybe they were waiting for Mishazzo to begin to trust him more.

He didn't tell them about the bottle. About sitting there dying for a piss, sure that as soon as he started, Mishazzo would reappear. He didn't tell them about smoking more than he'd ever smoked before, out of boredom. He didn't tell them about trying to think of things to write in the book, or how most of the things he thought of were things he would never write. His mind was dividing. Parts of it were roped off. There were things he could say. There were things he could not say but could write in the book. And now there were things he could neither say nor write but only think, and they pressed up against the others like they wanted a fight.

Hawthorn told him sometimes about other cases he was working on. A couple of murders. A robbery. Vague, no details. Sometimes Hawthorn asked him if he knew certain people. He named names. Most of them were unfamiliar. Once or twice there was one he thought he knew, but he said nothing.

– How come you know no one?

– I'm not . . .

– What?

He brushed the skin of his chest.

– I'm not a crook. I don't hang out with crooks.

Hawthorn said nothing for a while. He was smiling.

– What are you then?

– I just do the driving thing.

– And the pickpocketing thing. And the hotel thing.

– I rob, sometimes. Yeah. But I'm not a crook. I don't like crooks. I don't like all that. I stay away from it. I avoid those people.

– How are you going to get ahead?

– I don't want to get ahead.

Mishazzo asked him one day:

– Why are you looking in the mirror?

– I am?

– Are we being followed?

– No. I don't think so.

– So why?

– I didn't know I was looking in the mirror.

– You're looking in the mirror all the time.

– Sorry.

– That's OK. You know what to do if we're being followed?

– I tell you. I drive normally. I describe the car.

– Yes. If it happens, then we drive back to Tottenham. Back to the office. Nice and slow. Nice and normal. It will be police.

He nodded.

Mishazzo swayed his shoulders so that his head travelled from one edge of the mirror to the other.

– If it isn't police then what do you do?

Price had said that it would always be police. That no one else is that stupid.

– I don't know.

Mishazzo laughed.

– Then we call the fucking police my friend. We call 999 and you put your fucking foot down.

One day he counted up all the things he'd written. And he counted up all the things she had written. He had written more. More sentences, entries, whatever they were. He wasn't sure about words. Sometimes she wrote a whole page. Or more. Sometimes she drew little doodles, or pictures. Faces and flowers and a house with windows and a fence in the front and a path to the door, and the sun overhead. Her drawings were terrible, like an infant's. But he stared at them for ages. Once he started to draw something. A face, he thought. But it was a mess from the first mark he made and he scribbled it out.

He didn't tell Hawthorn about the book.

He thought that if she died, he would keep it. But he would destroy it before he died, and he would let no one else look at it. No one else in the world, ever, would read it. It would be something that had happened only for them, and when they were gone it would be something that had never happened.

That made him sad to the point of crying, almost, and he felt like an idiot.

One morning there was a man in the car with Mishazzo. This was not unusual. But this time Mishazzo did not want to go to a café. He wanted to be driven around.

– Drive east. Go toward the Olympics. I need to see what it looks like now. We can talk as we drive.

He could sense a pause as the other man gave Mishazzo a look.

– It's OK, Mishazzo said quietly. It's good.

They talked about cars. They talked about money. They talked about expanding something that was working well. The man mentioned a name. Gull. Gull, he said, wanted no splashback. They talked about money again. Mishazzo produced a little calculator from his briefcase and they added numbers. Small numbers. 86 plus 134, 17 divided by 5. The other man wrote down some of the numbers on a scrap of paper on his knee. They seemed then to be talking about hurting someone, but then they seemed to be talking simply about collecting someone. Or something. Then they were laughing about everything.

He drove around the Olympic fences, past the hoardings – the long colourful boards sometimes marked by graffiti. They couldn't really see anything. Mishazzo got bored and told him to turn around. In the back seat they were talking about music. Mishazzo wanted a CD played, then a different one, a specific song.

He braked sharply. He'd been fiddling with the CD player. There was a short silence. Then he apologized.

– My fault, said Mishazzo. I employ you to drive. Not to be my fucking DJ.

Mishazzo and the other man started to sing in the back seat. They sang songs they both knew in raucous, untuned voices and laughed, and he found himself laughing as well, and singing sometimes too when he knew the words or the tune.

The man handed him a roll of money when he got out of the car. It was nearly one hundred pounds in grubby fives and tens that smelled of his father's kitchen, and sweat, and ropes. Mishazzo told him to drive back to the office. That was it for the day.

– Now you see, he said. Now you see how dull my business is. But it pays well. And it makes you friends.

They lay next to each other in the bed and touched each other and laid their faces one against the other and when they were tired of talking they fucked and when they were tired of fucking they talked, and many different afternoons became one afternoon that persisted in his mind for the rest of his life and he never knew what to make of it, then or after.

– What does Mishazzo do?

– What?

– Mishazzo. Why are you interested in him? What does he do?

– You don't know?

– I know some.

Hawthorn didn't say anything.

– I know he does some buying and selling. Stolen cars.

Hawthorn nodded.

– I know he owns a couple of cafés.

– He does.

– They're just cafés.

– Yeah. They are.

– So what else does he do?

Hawthorn hummed and rubbed his nose.

– He owns two launderettes.

– I didn't know that.

– Yeah. The launderettes, the cafés. He owns that building in Tottenham.

– The office? I thought he rented.

– No. He's the landlord. Or maybe his daughter is.

– He has a daughter?

– He has two daughters. Their mother is dead.

– So what does he do?

– He provides. Largely speaking, that's what he does. He's a businessman. He talks. He makes deals. He negotiates. He opens up conversations with people running various . . . rackets, all over North London. He offers them things they might need. Resources. And he introduces people to other people. Broker. Provider. Facilitator.

He nodded. Mishazzo was a businessman. A talker. Like his father.

– It's tangled.

He wanted to ask Hawthorn how dangerous Mishazzo was. Whether he hurt people. Whether he got Price to hurt people. Whether that was part of business or whether it was all exaggerated.

– What laws has he broken then?

– All of them.

– He doesn't kill people.

Hawthorn looked at him suddenly, his eyes a bit wide.

– He doesn't kill people, he agreed.

– He doesn't?

– No.

They said no more about it. He didn't believe him.

Child looked at them. He looked at them and seemed to shut his eyes for a tiny moment. He looked from one to the other and seemed to pause, and shut his eyes. For a second. Two seconds. And then he muttered *Oh for fuck's sake*, and he went to the counter to pay for their coffees and Hawthorn's slice of cake and the bottle of water.

He never saw Child again.

Mishazzo stared at him. In the mirror. All he could see was the middle of Mishazzo's face. His eyes. Half of his forehead. His nose. His upper lip. Mishazzo said nothing. He didn't want music. They were driving to the café in Holloway. He looked sad. Depressed. As if he wanted to confide something.

– Your girl is good?

– Yes sir.

– What is her name?

– Mary, he lied.

– Mary?

Mishazzo laughed.

– She is a virgin?

He turned into Seven Sisters Road. The sun came through the passenger window and warmed his face. He did not want anything to go wrong.

– She has a job?

– Yes.

– What does she do?

– She's a receptionist.

Mishazzo nodded.

– Where is she a receptionist?

– At an estate agent's.

– Where?

– Oh. Down in the City.

– Down in the City. She likes that?

– Yes, I think so.

– You think so?

– She likes it. She likes working there. She likes the people. She likes being in the City.

– Commercial?

He looked in the mirror at Mishazzo's third of a face. He could tell nothing from it.

– What do you mean?

– Commercial property? Residential property?

– Residential.

Mishazzo's voice was impatient. Maybe it was the traffic. There wasn't much of it but it was veering all over the road.

He felt his face light up. His skin was hot on the left.

– Do you want me to stay on Seven Sisters?

– Why wouldn't you stay on Seven Sisters?

Mishazzo's eyes were on his left. Everything was burning up. He wanted to crash the car. For a second he thought about it. He could swerve suddenly, glance off the van on his inside, spin around, be hit by the approaching bus. He could skid off the road into railings. He could hurt himself if he did it hard enough. He could end up in a bed with people bringing him grapes and cards, watching TV all day, with her by his side.

He shifted in his seat so that the eyes were smaller. He drove with his shoulder pressed up against the door as if trying to open it.

He called Hawthorn. It went straight to his voicemail and he hung up.

He walked through the park. He tried Hawthorn again. Twice.

He sat at a bench and looked at some boys playing football. He called again and left a message.

– Call me please. As soon as you can.

She was at work. He could see the café from the bench. He stayed put. There were the boys playing football. There were some people walking. There were no parked cars.

She was surprised to see him.

– What's wrong?

– Nothing is wrong. I finished early. Thought I'd come over.

She took his arm and they walked along the canal for a while. She kept asking him what was wrong. He kept laughing and saying *Nothing. Nothing.*

Hawthorn called him back just as they got home.

– What is it?

– Nothing.

– Nothing?

– What time tomorrow?

– The usual. What's wrong?

He looked at his fingers and watched her close the curtains against the low sun. He felt that something awful was happening but he didn't know what, and he stared at her back in shadow and suspected that the feeling itself was the awful thing, and then she said something and he lost his train of thought and Hawthorn had hung up.

He waited early by the car, smoking, looking at the street. He wasn't thinking about anything. He didn't notice Price until he heard him. Price standing in the door of the café a couple of doors down from the office. They sat in there a lot of the time – Price and some of the others that he'd driven around. They sat there fiddling with their phones, reading the papers, annoying the waitress, doing whatever it was they did, coming and going.

– You avoiding me?

– What?

Price motioned to him. He glanced at the office, threw

down his cigarette, walked over.

– I never see you these days. You don't socialise. You don't come see me.

– Well, I'm working. It's been busy.

– Lots of busy. Hither and thither and yon. It's as good as The Knowledge.

He nodded. Price was smiling. All friendly, hands in pockets, rocking a little back and forth.

– How's the car? It need anything?

– It's fine.

– How's the missus?

He tensed, and his stomach did something, and he tried to look blank but he was sure he didn't.

– Who?

– Mary Mary, all contrary. The boss was telling me. You should come out at the weekend. To my place. Sunday afternoon. I have some of the lads over sometimes. Girlfriends, wives, kids. That sort of thing.

Price was wearing jeans. A blue jumper. He was smiling. He had his hands stuck halfway into his pockets.

– Don't look so fucking shocked, kid. It's a good thing. Wholesome. Family-friendly. Barbecue and drinks. Got a big plunge-pool thing for the kids. Watch out for Vinnie's missus after she's had a couple. You'll love it.

– Whereabouts?

– Near Braintree. Easy. You can take the car if you want I suppose. But probably better to hitch a lift with Pawel.

Teetotal. He doesn't live far from your place. Five minutes. Give or take.

– I said I'd see my father this weekend.

Price frowned.

– Don't bring your father, no offence.

– I mightn't be able to make it though.

Price rocked back and forth. Glanced to his left.

– You should come. You know, put on some friendly. It'd be smart. Let me know tomorrow.

Price nodded to his left.

– Your date is here.

Mishazzo was standing outside the office door looking at them, a little smile on his face, his umbrella clutched under his arm and his hands peeling the cellophane off a packet of cigarettes.

They drove all the way to Luton, not talking, listening to Ernest Carvallio's *Music Of The Barrios*, the smile on Mishazzo's face as constant as the road.

– Is there a procedure? For . . . if I get in trouble. What happens? What do you do?

Hawthorn rubbed his eyes. He smelled of a long day.

– You're a long way off anything like that.

– He knows where I live.

– Of course he knows where you live. What made you think he wouldn't know where you live? You probably told him where you live. When you went there first.

– No.

– Your father then.

He said nothing. He sipped his coffee. He bounced his fucking knee and he looked out the fucking window.

– So you won't help us?

– You don't need help. You're panicking. You're being stupid. They are not suspicious. They like you. They're being friendly.

He tried to tell her to tie him tighter. To hit him harder. To yank his head back by the hair. He wanted her to spit in his face, in his mouth. He wanted her to hit him. But he was no good at talking. He tried to make her guess things by the way he reacted. She seemed to get it. But not enough. She was too careful, too considerate. She checked too much. He thought about writing it in the book. Like instructions. But the book was not for that.

Price called him on the Friday.

– Don't need you today after all.

– No?

– I'll pay you half.

– OK.

– You coming on Sunday?

– Sure.

– Good boy. I'll get Pawel to pick you up about midday. What's the girlfriend's name again?

He looked at the curtain. The day was making it bulge. She had gone to work. He pressed his thumb against a bruise on his ribs.

– Mary.

– Right. Mary. Informal. Bring a bottle.

And he hung up. Without asking for the address. Not even which number flat. Nothing.

– You're not going to help us.

Hawthorn sighed again.

– What do you want me to do?

– Money. At least some money.

– For what?

– To get away.

Hawthorn laughed.

– Where are you going to go?

– Morocco.

– Morocco. What are you talking about?

– Or Spain. Morocco or Spain.

Hawthorn crossed his arms. He looked like he was going to cry, but his body was angry and his voice was cold and he was laughing at him. They sat in Hawthorn's kitchen, at Hawthorn's table. He felt like he had never been there before.

– You want to run away to Morocco or Spain because a couple of dodgy geezers have invited you to a barbecue?

Hawthorn's voice was quiet. There was a shake in it. He couldn't tell if it was laughter or anger.

Fuck. Fuck it.

He tried to hit Hawthorn. He threw his left arm out – why his left arm he didn't know, all his strength was in the right – and Hawthorn simply leaned away from it, and it glanced off his shoulder, maybe his ear, and Hawthorn had stood and his chair was clattering to the floor, and he had stood up too, apparently, and he threw the right and Hawthorn caught it, and something hit his stomach and he clenched, and then Hawthorn was smothering him, his arms around him, clamping him down so that he could not hit again, couldn't raise his hands, and he tried to butt with his head and break the hold, but he was just jerking in Hawthorn's arms like a crying child and he could hear sobs, and he looked for the door, he just wanted the door, and he struggled and he shouted *Let me fucking go*, and he had made no impact at all, none, and they broke from each other and he could not look back, and there was just a simple gap where there had previously been something complicated. On the stairs he wiped his cheeks but they were dry.

She was watching television. He stood in the doorway. Eventually she looked back at him.

– What is it?

– We have to go.

– What?

– Pack, he said. Quickly.

She stared at him. He could see her start to feel afraid.

It was the way he looked.

– *EastEnders*, she said, very quietly.

– Pack. Now. Not much. Basic stuff. Money. Passport. Some clothes. We might not be back . . . for a while.

– What the fuck?

– Just do it.

He went to the bedroom. He threw things on the bed. Clothes. He couldn't think. He pulled bags from the top of the wardrobe. He took the shoebox from the bottom drawer, tipped it out on the dresser. Her passport, his, the other half of his drivers' licence, a credit card he never used, some euro notes. He stopped. He took off his shoes, his jeans. He walked back into the living room. She was on the phone.

– Who are you talking to?

– My mother.

He didn't know what to say.

– Tell her you'll call her tomorrow.

He went to the bathroom. He took off the rest of his clothes and switched on the shower. He was sweating. He stepped in and stood under the water and he thought about trains. Trains, hotels, money. He thought through all of it again. He knew he wasn't thinking straight, but he didn't know how to fix that. After a few minutes she came in.

– Where are we going?

– Paris.

– What's happened?

– I'll tell you when we get going. Please go and pack.

When he got out she was still there.

– It's OK, he said. Everything will be OK. Just fucking pack, will you.

– You have to tell me.

– I fucked up. Stay if you want to. I have to leave. I'm going in about ten minutes.

He walked, dripping, through to the bedroom. In the doorway he froze. It took him a second or two to realize that it hadn't been ransacked, that he'd made the mess himself.

In the taxi she called her mother and told her they were flying to Barcelona for a couple of days on a cheap last-minute deal. At St Pancras they had to rush. It hadn't cost much, he told her. He ran up the escalators with both their bags. He could hear himself wheezing. Cigarettes. They had two seats facing the wrong way. When they were settled he kissed her. Then he told her. He told her about Mishazzo, that he was a big deal. He told her about the violence. How they went and beat people up. He told her about Price. He told her about the gunshot. He told her about the two policemen who had picked him up by the Emirates. He told her about the deal they gave him. This was the story. He told her about the hotel jobs. He told her that he'd had no choice. He told her that Price was a psycho. He told her that the cops were psychos too. He told her that Price had become suspicious. He didn't know why. Maybe he'd heard something. That the cops were talking to someone. He didn't know. Price was on to him, he thought. He'd tried to keep her out of it. But Price knew where they lived.

– I didn't tell them anything about you. Nothing true. They think you work at an estate agent's. They think you're called Mary.

– What the fuck?

– They fucking kill people. You understand? They kill people. I'm driving this guy around and I'm telling the cops where I take him and he has people beaten up, killed. You understand that? This is the fucking story.

He was speaking through his teeth, trying to be quiet. Around them were couples just like them. Couples went to Paris on the train – it was what they did.

She wanted to know why he hadn't told her about the hotels. Then she wanted to know more about the violence. She wanted to know what Mishazzo did.

– He's a businessman. Resources. He puts people together.

– What are you talking about? What resources?

He told her about the cars.

– He steals cars?

– No. He sells them on. Stolen. Or he trades them. That's part of it.

– What's the other part of it?

– I don't know. He's a broker.

– A broker?

He nodded.

– What the fuck is a broker?

He told her again about the shot. About Mishazzo's face in the rear-view mirror. He mangled things. They sounded slight in his mouth, like nothing. Like he made them up. But this was what was happening to them. They had to get away because of what mattered. And nothing else mattered. Why couldn't she see?

He stopped suddenly. The book. He remembered the book. He had left it. It had slipped his mind. He stopped talking in the middle of a sentence and he looked at her. Jesus.

– What?

– The book.

He could not feel them moving. He could feel nothing. He was encased in something, buried in something, smothered or drowning. His hand was shaking and he could not focus his eyes and he stared at her for a second and then he could not see her.

She moved towards him as if he was disappearing, and her face became something he could see, and she reached out to him and she held his head.

– I have it. I have it.

She made him look at her.

– I have it. It's in my bag. I have it.

He breathed out but could not breathe in. He let himself slump against her. There was no relief. He fell down inside himself. He had forgotten it. He had run and left it behind. He had run. All those words.

How To Have Fun
With A Fat Man

The men are solemn and he wants to laugh. They stand singly or in small groups, by the wall, waiting for the action to begin. The thump of the beat is not so loud here. But the air is dense and viscid and connects them to each other, so that he feels a man could push him over without touching him.

There are certain things Hawthorn wants to do. There are things he doesn't want to do. The line between these things tickles him, like the bead of sweat down his back. His mind imagines situations. Certain situations. Certain possible conjunctions. Certain pictures arise in his mind, and he flits from the pictures to the scene in front of him, and constructs paths from here to there, across the pulse of the drums and the thick air. He doesn't trust his mind.

He knows how it's supposed to be done.

At a signal they move away from the wall. They move towards the others. It is always a confrontation. It is always a standoff. Hawthorn is shoulder to shoulder with men like himself.

He is eye to eye across the air. He is picking out certain faces. He is making calculations. There are certain things he wants to do. There are things he doesn't want to do. These things are always people. He accepts or declines each face. Each set of shoulders. He is agreeing to and refusing each body in turn. His mind is ahead of him. He is saying yes to that one, no to that one. He is choosing. Choice is an illusion.

He pulls the strap on his helmet. He adjusts the grip on his shield.

He opens the towel around his waist and pulls it a little tighter and ties it again, tucking one edge of it under another, breathing in, his shoulders lifting and falling against the wall.

There is a man he wants nothing to do with. There are things he doesn't want to do. He manoeuvres to avoid. He aligns his body just so. He exerts pressure in a different direction. The music. And with it, out of mouths all around him, noises prior to language. Movement from before language. Everything here is before language. How can his mind help him with that?

He feels a hand on him. He doesn't know how it's connected. He feels a face next to his. He doesn't know whether the hand and the face are linked, how to see them, how to know if what he wants is anything to do with it any more. He pushes. He pushes harder. There is another hand on him, or maybe it is the same hand.

A voice crackles in his earpiece and they hold a line. There is a smell of sweat and the heat shimmers above the bodies in front of him and they swirl like they are simmering, cooking, about to boil, and the man beside him shouts something that Hawthorn can make no sense of but for its excited anger and its eagerness, and he feels his heart thumping and is surprised and immediately not surprised to find that he has an erection.

He feels a mouth on him. He thinks it is a mouth. In the soft dark his cock is being sucked by someone he cannot see. He tries to decipher shapes. Hands are on him. He doesn't know whose hands. He closes his eyes. There is a shape by his shape, a high sweet smell, a cock pressing against his thigh. He takes the cock in his hand. He cannot see anything. He opens his eyes. There are shapes and sounds. He tries to see shapes behind the sounds. No one uses language. He cannot see the fat man. He pulls his hips back gently, puts his hand on the head that is sucking him, makes it stop. It is doing it too well. There is too much to do. He sinks to his knees to see what will happen. He is presented with two cocks, and he sucks one and holds the other. He moans and the darkness tumbles around him and he moves his hands above his head. There are flat bodies. He closes his eyes. He is swimming in the river and the river is on his skin. He is partaking of a comfort that predates anything his mind might think about it.

He feels a hand on his cock somehow. He smiles towards a laugh, and has to pause his sucking. His pause is taken for something else, and the cock in front of his mouth disappears and is replaced by its obverse and the cock to his left becomes a pair of helping hands and he is back on the riverbank with the scent of the earth and the rough close clamp of the soil, and he declines, in this dark, just now, amongst strangers, and he stands up grinning.

The crowd surges and they hold the line. Faces are roaring at him. At him personally. Some of the faces are the sort of thing he expects. Others seem too young and fresh for this. Or too old and smart. Too cunning. He can feel the pressure on his shield, and it all comes through his hands. He adjusts his feet to lean forward, to take some of the strain off his arms. It brings his face closer to their faces. They can't see his face though. They see his helmet and his chin strap and his neck guard and his eyes. They all look him in the eye. Every face he turns to seeks out his eyes. He blinks.

There is a roar to his left, localized, and the line seems to break for an instant. There is a uniform on the ground, and the focus is suddenly there, everyone is staring at the man down, man down, and the crowd wheels around him. In his helmet he laughs. Man down.

*

The fat man is still there. He stands against the wall, and Hawthorn sees only his shape – a bulge of cold grey with a whiter band around his middle, like something ready for the oven. Hawthorn is having his cock sucked by a skull with a buzz cut on top of hard shoulders, and he is trying not to come. Another man is investigating his arse. He laughs out loud. The sucking man mistakes this for a signal, and moves his head back and uses his hand instead, which Hawthorn taps with his own, and everything winds down. *Taking a break*, he says, smiling, and is not sure whether he has said it out loud or not. He goes towards the showers.

They have their orders. In his earpiece he hears the calm voice. They stand, they stay, they move, they wheel, they retreat. Someone is playing them like snooker. Moving them around like an arm. He waits for a bottle to hit him. None do. They fall short. They hit others. He stands there, in a trained stance, braced.

Hawthorn's father brought drinks out to the garden. His brother was fussing over his son, Hawthorn's nephew. Hawthorn scratched his cheek and smiled at his father and took the beer.

    – How's work?

    – It's all right.

    – Still with Child?

    – Still with Child, yes.

His father laughed. Hawthorn smiled and nodded. His brother was talking about sweets.

– Close as you'll ever get to making me a grandfather again.

All the old jokes. His father liked it.

– John and Tess are the ones you need to talk to about that.

– Don't even think about it, said his brother grimly, fixing his son's shoe. They laughed. The boy wanted to know why.

– What? What? Tell me.

– Go annoy your sister.

He glared at them all and ran off. Tess came out of the house, still on her phone. She walked behind Hawthorn and ran her hand across his shoulders. The sun was warm and the beer was good. He looked at his father. He was still handsome. He looked strong and healthy. John was getting fat. He had the pear shape of a cabby and his mother's smile.

Hawthorn squinted. Rubbed his eyes. He put on his sunglasses.

– Are you ever in uniform these days? Tess said to him. She was off the telephone. She was looking at him as she poured herself another glass of wine.

– No, not working. Just functions. Formal things. I had to wear it to a funeral the other week.

– I miss it. The uniform.

– Who died? his father asked.

– I didn't know him. Ex-detective. Retired I mean. Fairly young still. Fifties.

– You were always handsome in the uniform. Wasn't he, John?

– What did he die of?

– He drowned.

– He drowned?

– On holiday in . . . the Canaries. I think. Went in the sea somewhere odd, you know. Somewhere he shouldn't have. Got in trouble.

– Suicide?

– Nah, don't think so. There was no talk of it.

– I know a guy who drowned in the Canaries and all.

Hawthorn looked at his brother. He expected a joke. But John sipped his beer, waiting to be asked.

– Go on then. Who?

– Cabby. Freddie . . . something. Freddie Cohen or something. Big guy. Quiet guy. Nice man. But quiet, you know. Nervous type. Daytime driver only, ever. Nervous shy guy. Not what you'd expect from looking at him. Big belly, Jewfro, great big bushy beard. Gentle giant sort. Weakling really. Anyway. It wasn't Cohen. I can't remember what it was. Anyway. He went to the Canaries with his wife, and his two brothers and their wives, and a plane full of kids and the elderly mother and half of Stamford Hill or whatever. And they had practically a whole floor of some seaside hotel, and every morning they annexed a big section of beach with rugs and blankets and picnic baskets and sunshades and god knows. Kids' toys, clothes, hampers, whole bloody extended family support system and paraphernalia. So one morning, Freddie is wandering from the little showers, you know the little stand-alone shower nozzles they have at the edge of a beach, and he's been sitting in the sun and he's sweated a bit – fat Freddie – and he's just taken a turn under the shower thing, and he's wandering back towards the hotel for his morning shit when

– John.

– No, he was – it's part of the story. He needs a shit. So he's walking back to the hotel, and he's all wet, and he's got a towel thrown around his shoulders, but he's barefoot, on those poolside tiles, he's left his flip-flops by the shower. And he slips. You know. He just goes arse over tit. And he lands on his side and rolls into the pool. And there's a great big splash, and all the kids in the pool are laughing, and some of the people who've seen it think it's the funniest thing they've ever seen. It's *You've Been Framed* stuff. If anyone had caught it. So there's a lot of laughter. But then the laughter just stops. 'Cos suddenly there's this plume of something in the water. You know, a big stain of something in the water. And for a second everyone thinks it's blood, and the kids all dash for the sides and climb out, screaming, and the grown-ups stand up and come over. They think it's blood. But then they notice that if it's blood it's clotting already, in these little clumps . . .

– Oh Christ.

– Yeah. It's not blood. It's not red. It's brown. Poor Freddie's had such a shock that he's shit himself. Big Freddie. On his holidays. He's eating what he likes, you know, for once, and he's full to overflowing with last night's five courses; garlic mushrooms, pickled herring, I don't know, meatballs, chocolate ice cream . . .

– John! Stop it. That's disgusting.

– It's what happened. Anyway. Poor Freddie. And it's foreign food. So he's a bit, you know. Loose.

– Jesus Christ, John.

– And people are standing around, you know. At least, some men are. The kids have all run off, and the mothers are gathering them in, checking for flecks, all that. For new moles. And there's some guys standing at the edge just looking at the water and it's only after a little while that someone asks, where is he? Why hasn't he surfaced? And they're peering down there, under the water, and they can see him. They can see the shape. They can see his bulk, and the Jewfro, and his big blue shorts. It's like the shit is a pyramid in the water, an upside down pyramid, and at its point, there's Freddie's ballooned-out blue shorts. Just hovering there. Treading water. Under water. So they begin to think maybe he's stuck. Maybe he's got his foot caught in a drain or a grill or something – you know you hear about that happening. And they're all looking at each other 'cos they know that one of them is going to have to go in there. Into the shit. To get him out.

– Oh John, this is awful.

– Have I not told you this before?

– No!

– Well. OK. So one guy, a young guy, he decides he'll go in.

He'll do it. So he moves away from the shit a little bit, to clearer water, and he puts on his goggles, and he closes his mouth and holds his nose and slides in. And when he's underwater he waits for the bubbles to clear and he looks over towards Freddie. Big Freddie. He's standing there, or floating, and all the water around him is dark and full of bits of shit and at his legs, near his middle, there's this big cloud of liquid shit, just floating there, and Freddie has his back to the wall of the pool, his arms over his head, pressed against the underside of the bar, the rail, stopping himself from surfacing. He's holding himself under. And the guy looks at him, you know, like, what the hell is he doing? And he waves at him. And Freddie looks over. And Freddie has this look on his face. This grim sort of terrified look of shame. Pure shame. He looks at the guy, and he looks away again immediately. He can't look at him. Can't look. He just shakes his head furiously. As if to say, you know, don't look at me, leave me alone, leave me.

– Oh my God, the poor man.

– Yeah.

– They got him out, right?

– You try shifting a big man like Freddie out from underwater when he doesn't want to be shifted. While everything is slick with shit as well, and he's got his arms rammed rigid against the rail. Anyway. The interesting thing is that it took forever for the guy who'd got in the water to get anyone else to help him. They wouldn't even reach in to try and pry Freddie's hands of the rail for ages. The guy, the young guy, he bobs up to the surface, and he tells them what's going on, but they all just sort of stand there looking at him.

– He drowned?

– He drowned.

Hawthorn looked at his brother closely.

– Come on.

– What?

– This is a Jew joke. I'm waiting for the punchline.

His brother opened his mouth and looked at him.

– Jesus. It was a horrible death. Why would it be a Jew joke? He was Jewish. What can I do about that? You're telling me you haven't had weird deaths on your beat? I know you have. You've had weirder than that. It's not a joke. It just happened. Freddie Simon. I think. Something like that. Look it up.

Their father laughed. They both looked at him. He shrugged. Sipped his beer. His granddaughter ran over and whispered something to her mother. Tess stood up and walked to the house with her, hand in hand.

– Anyway, said John. Just goes to show.

Hawthorn thought the punchline was coming then. With Tess out of the way. He waited for it. Something about floating Jews, drowning Jews, Jews and shit, something like that. John said nothing. Then he stood up and stretched and went off to play with his boy.

– I swear that's a joke.

– What's the punchline?

– I don't know. We've embarrassed him out of telling us.

– John doesn't do embarrassed.

– He's getting fat himself. Maybe he's embarrassed about that.

His father laughed.

– He's not fat. Jesus. No one in this family gets fat. Not on my side anyway. He's just settled a little. He sits all the time. Needs more golf. If you weren't walking around half of London all day long you'd be fat, the crap you eat. When I was a kid you never saw a fat person. Or if you did you ran home and told your mum about it. These days everyone is fat as fools. It's the crap they eat. So much crap. You see them, the kids, stuffing their faces. Fat little kids. Your mother fed you right. If you weren't a cop you'd have ruined all that by now.

– I thought no one in this family got fat.

– You have fat skin.

– I have what?

– Bad skin. Unhealthy. You have a pallor. You're not getting the right vitamins or something. Circles under your eyes.

Hawthorn sighed.

– You need looking after, his father said, a little quietly.

Then,

– You get Jew jokes at work?

– We get all sorts of jokes at work. Everyone gets their turn.

– Gay jokes?

– Lots of gay jokes.

– You complain?

He smiled.

– What do you think?

– They funny?

– Some of them.

– Like what? Tell me a few. I love a good fag joke.

He looked at his father, sitting with his hand on his beer bottle, healthy, his body relaxed in the sun. He was in shape. His eyes were two living rivets in a hard shell, his face the summary of an argument, lined with a lifetime of being right. His knee bounced slightly. He tossed his chin minutely towards the sky and stared, smiling.

– Fuck off, Dad.

His father laughed at him. Laughed loud and loosely, and folded his body forward a little and slapped him on the shoulder.

He clamps his hand to his flat stomach, his little finger finding his navel, and he slides along the wet wall, moving to his left, towards a man with a tattoo on his arm that is vibrant and glistening in the half light like a wound.

In the crowds around Bank, the woman with the green parka and the torn jeans has been like a catch on the movement of his eyes. He keeps on seeing her. Her face is raised out from the blur of other faces. She carries no sign. But she snarls an ugly anger that distorts her features into something crooked and unnatural and he is drawn to her and knows it, and tries to lose her in the noise and the chaos, but she always seems there when he looks, and there as well when he looks away.

He is fucking some guy in the dark. His towel over his shoulders, his head back, his eyes closing and opening, everything coming at him through his cock and his hands. He is distracted by the music, by its beat. He is trying not to match it. Some other man is there. He thinks about taking the guy he's fucking to a private cabin. He thinks about coming or not coming. Everything is possible. He runs his hands over his own body. He slaps the guy's arse. He presses his hand to the man's back, all bone and muscle. He concentrates on containment. On keeping things from getting out of hand.

There is a burst of drums in front of him, a sudden clatter in the steady rhythm, as if something's fallen over. Heads flick to the left. There is a new line of men behind him. Everything rattles in the near distance. Focus comes and goes. Everywhere he looks he seems to have just missed something. OK. There are two lines of men behind him now. He leans on his neighbour, who looks at him. He reaches down to pull a knee pad tighter. A plastic bottle hits his shield. He looks up. The first face he sees is covered by a black scarf and hood. It sits on a small plump body. He can see the eyes looking at him. Piggy eyes. Stupid fucking piggy eyes. He shouts into his helmet. He is gone from himself and he knows it and he thinks about going back but he doesn't really want to.

*

The dark moves and he lets it move over him and he doesn't care. He isn't fucking anyone now. He is in the half dark on a soft pallet. He is kissing a man with a beard. The man has a beautiful mouth, a relaxed way of kissing, a stillness in his shoulder muscles. The music is quieter. Or he has lost it. It doesn't matter. There are others.

All the men move forward. He hears a laugh somewhere behind him. His eyes are on the same eyes. He steps on the bottle. They will meet now. The lines. They will touch. They will press up against each other. All the anticipation will rebound on them and there will be a kind of sigh, a relief. A sort of love. He laughs. He still has his erection. It presses against his belt or something, and there is a marvellous sharp discomfort that makes him moan. He shouts into his helmet. He loses the eyes. There is a stir of faces. They meet. The lines. There is a sigh, a relief, nothing happens. There's a hush. As if everyone is suddenly a bit embarrassed.

He finds himself being caressed, on the back, the hips. The kissing is doing him a lot of good. He would be happy to have it continue for a long time. There is a pause. He opens his eyes. The man with the beard is kissing another. The fat man. Hawthorn looks at him. His fat shoulders and his fat arms. His chins. The fat of his chest. The fat man has his hand on Hawthorn's arse. Hawthorn pushes it away. He reaches for the bearded man's cock, and sets his shoulder sideways.

The whistles somehow get through everything else and someone to his left strikes out at one of them and there is a tight scuffle and he sets his feet steady, pushes, feels the men behind him push against his back, lean into him. He is behind his shield. A face appears and spits at him. Another does the same. He is looking through a film of saliva. He swings his truncheon upwards from underneath and it hits something soft, but he can see no reaction on the selection of faces in front of him so he pulls it back, goes again. It hits something hard and there is a cry, but he cannot see which face has made it. He extracts his arm and brings it over his head and leaves it there. A face says 'Ooooooh' in a camp voice, and laughs at him. He finds those eyes and stares at them and they falter and the face turns away.

The fat man's body is disgusting. Parts of it brush against Hawthorn. There is more of him. Too much to avoid. He rolls and quivers and his shape heaves itself like a sea, and his face is sickly sweet and grinning in the half dark like a giant child's face, slurping, kissing the bearded man all wrong, and his belly spreads across Hawthorn's like a flood, and Hawthorn feels small and brittle and on the verge of something. He pushes at the weight, and his hands are like sticks in sand. This is not like him.

*

He finds the piggy eyes again. The arsehole eyes. The hood is fallen back now, and the hair is buzzed short like Hawthorn's. The scarf still covers the mouth. Hawthorn pushes the button, speaks, describes the fat boy. He has to repeat his number three times. He has to describe the boy twice. Someone tells him to move that way, to push out. He pushes. He roars and pushes. He shouts. He remembers the button and stops shouting. The men on either side follow him. He holds the piggy eyes in his. The eyes dart a little. They snap back to Hawthorn, hold for a second. He gets the impression that they're smiling. Then the hood comes back up and the piggy head ducks and disappears. Shit. The men are still at his shoulder. He pushes his button. He is about to redirect them all when he sees a short-haired girl in front of him with a sneering face and a black scarf around her neck and a red hoodie. *Red hoodie*, he shouts. He grabs her. She hits his arm. He brings his truncheon down on her shoulder, hard. The men at his side clear a space. He holds her again, by the fabric on her chest. She is screaming. A boy is trying to protect her. Hawthorn sees him hit from the side by a shield edge. His head snaps backward, and falls forward again, dripping blood. Hawthorn drags the girl towards him. She is half crouched, half sitting. He wants to drag her by her hair but her hair is short like a boy's. She is crying. She wears tight black jeans and her nose is pierced and he can see a tattoo on the skin of her hip where her clothes have parted. Everything about her makes Hawthorn furious. He drags her for a few yards.

Someone comes to him, touches his arm. They lift her between them and walk her towards the arrest point. She is clutching her shoulder where he hit her, and she is sobbing, weeping, and looking behind her, for her boyfriend, crying.

– Fuck off, Hawthorn hissed.

  – What?

  – Fuck off, I said. Go lose some fucking weight.

They both looked at him.

The bearded man smiled.

  – Who's he talking to?

  – You, obviously.

  – You sure?

  – Well it can't be me, can it?

  – I think he's talking to both of us.

  – I think he is.

They turned away from him and faced each other. Something in his arm jerked and he had to bite to stop it. He pulsed. He let it recede. He turned around and left the room. He went and stood in the shower. He stayed there.

Later they make fun of him.

  – Whorethorn thought he'd got himself some nice fucking anarchist cock.

  – Whorethorn was hoodwinked by a titless dyke.

  – Whorethorn loves the smell of testosterone in the mornings.

– Whorethorn's got a hard-on for truncheon fucking.

– Whorethorn is a fucking fascist faggot.

He sat in his brother's garden watching the kids. He called out to them.

– Where's your paddling pool?

The boy shrugged.

– Dunno, said the girl.

– Will we find it? Set it up? It's hot enough.

The kids looked at each other. The girl frowned.

– I don't think so, said the boy.

They went on with whatever it was they were doing. Something with plastic blocks and the seat from the broken swing. They talked to each other quietly so that he couldn't hear. His brother and Tess were in the kitchen getting the dinner ready. His father was watching the second half of the match.

He didn't know what to do.

He thought about faking a phone call and going home.

He thought about going to the sauna. He hadn't been in months.

The kids were skinny and they looked like his brother when he'd been their age. Hawthorn watched them. He remembered going with his brother to the swimming pool. He remembered them holding their breath. They would duck underwater and see who could hold their breath the longest. He had forgotten. It was something they did. He remembered being under the water, with his goggles on, looking at his brother a foot or two away from him, both of them by the wall, with their hands on the bar, holding themselves under, staring at each other, not breathing, waiting, and waiting, and not breathing; looking at his brother's mouth, seeing a bubble escape; waiting, waiting, waiting. He couldn't remember surfacing. Only his brother's face, changing. Waiting.

He watched the kids; breathed out.

How We Ran The Night

Trainer told me this story.

– Ashid lives in Walthamstow, somewhere around there, east, used to be a steward at White Hart Lane years ago. Anyway, now he works further north, up outside the M25 somewhere, for a bloke called Palmer, who has this garage. Called Mastersons, for no reason I know of. They beat panels, they cut and splice, pull apart, put together. They spray-paint. Most of their business is stolen cars. They have an arrangement with a man called Gull. Ashid's role is mainly paperwork. A clever man with documents. Log books, bills of sale, transfer records, service records, repair reports. He does the accounts as well. Various accounts. The presentable and the bottom drawer, you know.

– So. All is well. They're making a living. They keep an eye out. They pay careful attention to visitors they don't know. They hire a local boy, they hire his brother, they pay them well, look after them, tell them nothing very much. They are circumspect. Canny. Smart as old goats. Palmer and Ashid. They're never stupid. Never rash. Gull is happy. Every Christmas he gives each of them a hamper. Things for the kids. He remembers birthdays. Every so often little gifts – watches, computers, holidays. He will call Ashid on a Thursday, tell him that there are tickets at the airport for him and his wife, that there is a hotel booked in Cyprus or Budapest or Paris – go, have fun, have a good time, send me a postcard. Ashid always goes. He never says no. He's a careful man.

– One day, one cold day in the winter, one afternoon, in January, in the bitter cold, Ashid is alone at the garage. He's doing the paperwork for a car that's come in the previous night. A four-wheel drive. A Land Rover. Palmer is out, he's not there, he's off somewhere on business. The yard is locked, the gates are secured, because of the Land Rover, which has been painted, which has had various changes made to the interior – it's new, it's about two weeks out of factory, it couldn't be newer, and it's sitting there, jacked up in the air, without wheels, without plates. Ashid needs to read some numbers from the engine. Some serial numbers. On various parts. He needs to know what they are before he decides what they will be. The boy has gone home early. Ashid can't remember why. The boy plays football. He's always going to football matches, maybe that's it. His brother is sick at home. There is flu and there are various other winter ailments. Ashid's wife is at home coughing, complaining about a draft in the bedroom at night. Their new windows, from Gull. They don't all fit. Ashid has arranged for someone to come and fix them.

– He sighs and lies down on the flat trolley and slides himself under the Land Rover. He has a torch and a pen and a notebook. He's not sure he'll be able to see all the numbers he wants to see from here. He'll have to wait until it's off the jacks before he can get all of them.

– He hears a sound. He hears it but he doesn't notice it. There are always sounds.

– He shines the torch up on the underside and sees a small plate to his left and squints at it, because the lettering is very small. He squints at it and it seems to come closer, and it does come closer. It comes closer because the whole Land Rover has come closer, it has fallen off its jacks, which is impossible, and it has crashed down on top of Ashid, knocking the pen and the torch and the notebook from his hands and pinning him to the ground. For a second he thinks he is dead. But he isn't dead. There's enough room beneath the Land Rover. It does not crush him. It has not fallen all the way. Then for a second he thinks he's holding it up, because his arms are above his head somehow, and the underside of the vehicle is pressing against his elbows. But of course he knows he's not holding it up. But he can't move his arms. And he's trapped.

– His mobile phone is in his trouser pocket but he can't move his arms. There's no one else in the garage. The garage is in the corner of a half-abandoned industrial estate. There is a plastics workshop at the other end. Out of shouting distance. There is a scrapyard where they sometimes hide cars, but that is even further away. On the other side of the yard wall there is simply open ground, waste ground, and then the trees start.

– He hears a voice. Close to him. Far too close to him. Palmer is his best hope but this isn't Palmer. Palmer isn't back. For a moment he cannot understand this voice. It seems too quiet, or too loud, too close, as if it is coming from a mouth that is beside his head. It is a low whispering voice, it sounds foreign, it's unsettling, odd, as if the voice of someone unused to speaking.

– *The vehicle will fall, fully, shortly, and you will be killed. It is prevented from falling by a small amount of metal, upon which the weight of the vehicle rests, but this small piece of metal is slipping, and the vehicle will fall, and because the wheels are off, the full weight of it will fall on you and you will undoubtedly be killed.*

– Ashid doesn't know what to say. He whimpers. He thinks that maybe this is God talking to him. Or maybe it's part of himself. Maybe he is so close to death that part of him is already dead and this part of him is talking to him from the other side of death, telling him calmly what to expect. He feels very cold. He's worried about pain. He finds that he is pressing his elbows painfully into the underside of the Land Rover. He realizes that this is ridiculous and he tries to stop doing it, but he's afraid that if he relaxes his arms he will die.

– *Save me*, is what he says. *Save me.* He doesn't even know if there is really someone there who can hear him or whether he is now praying, for the first time since childhood, or whether he is talking to the dead part of himself and in fact asking for death to come and save him.

– *We can save you*, says the strange voice, with no hesitation. And this confuses Ashid. He can hear only one voice, but now that he thinks about it, the voice sounds like it might be more than one voice, speaking at exactly the same time, with exactly the same inflections and emphasis and melody, and he says *Save me* again, and this time he is definitely speaking to whoever is speaking to him, and he hopes, he has hope.

– *First*, says the voice, say the voices, *you must promise us something.*

– *Anything*, says Ashid.

– *You must hear our story. We will tell you our story. You must listen to our story. You must listen to all of it. From the start at the old sun, to the end at the black ditch. You must listen to the tale of Estator and his brethren, to the story of their lives, and you must hear the tale of Whigs and Haft. You must listen to it all. From start to finish. You must remember it all. From start to finish. And you must set it down so that it is known.*

At this point Trainer stopped talking. He looked at his sirloin. Sniffed it. Poked it around the plate with his fork. He ordered more tea. We were in a café in Hackney. He didn't eat any of the steak. I think he'd ordered it as a sort of joke. Rare and bloody on a white plate.

– It is unknown, he said, and then paused. It is uncertain, debated, in dispute, as to whether Ashid heard the story of Estator at this point, while still trapped beneath the Land

Rover. Or whether he was saved first and was then told the story. What is known is that Palmer returned to the garage to find the Land Rover belly down on the floor of the yard, with the jacks buckled and crushed, and Ashid nowhere to be seen. Palmer called in the boys, sick or not, football or not, and they lifted the car, they winched it up, Palmer expecting to see the crushed body of his friend, but there was only the snapped flat trolley, a torch, a pen and a notebook. And a smell, like dogs or donkeys.

Ashid disappeared for two weeks. Neither his family nor his friends, nor Palmer, nor Gull, nor anyone, heard a word from him or saw or laid eyes on him or caught a glimpse of even his shadow, anywhere across all of North London. The police were not informed, as Gull expressed a certain nervousness at the idea. To make up for the lack of an official search, Gull utilized all of his not inconsiderable resources to track Ashid. But he turned up nothing. Nothing at all. His friends knew nothing, and then his enemies knew nothing, and why would they lie? They're businessmen like him. They're not wild gangsters. They're not TV-show baddies. They're calm, conservative men, and they like a mystery as little as he does.

And then he reappears. He comes home one morning, and his crying wife can get nothing out of him. And she calls Palmer. And Palmer calls Gull, but Ashid will see no one.

Trainer was pale. He looked at the door a lot.

He pushed a large envelope across the table.

*

My living room overlooks the park. As does my office. At night I see men in the bushes by the north railings. In all weathers. I see dogs roam the open spaces. Sometimes there is a human with a leash hovering nearby. Sometimes there isn't. I see lost children, regularly, wandering in the same few square feet, crying inconsolably. Even after a parent reappears, dashing down the paths for a hug, the child continues crying.

Trainer is a strange man.

The manuscript is almost damp, as if it's been left outside. Some of the pages are curled and stained, and they don't sit down pat on top of each other. They are much more like loose leaves. The whole thing smells. It's in Times New Roman though, double spaced. There are no marks, no corrections. The stains are tea and coffee and grass and earth and god knows. A few pages are torn, ragged, but everything is legible. It has the feel of something treated, weathered, aged – to serve the text.

HOW WE RAN THE NIGHT

An executive memoir by Estator, Prince of Wolves

Jesus Christ.

There is a secret London apparently, hidden in plain view, populated by wolves and ravens and wild dogs and foxes and a network of rats, and other, stranger animals, and by the people – the humans – who communicate and work with and profit from the tumult. There are tensions, moments of violence, battles, alliances, pacts, treaties. There is peace, subterfuge, balance, chaos, war. There are two religions and a dozen sects. There is a lineage of wolves stretching back to the early twelfth century.

An occasional car crawls around the crescent sometimes in the middle of the night, looking for business of one sort or another I assume. I don't think there's anything like that. I have seen foxes, of course.

I am almost unspeakably bored with every aspect of my life.

Estator, it seems, is a noble sort of wolf. He lives, he tells us, in the gaps, with his fellows. His fellow wolves. They live in the gaps between things. Buildings. Motorways. Where we don't look, I presume, is the point. Why is it that these things are always filled with snow and moonlight? Meetings on bridges. Rooftops. Frozen lakes. The chief currency appears to be honour.

It is very badly written.

What on earth is an 'executive memoir' anyway? I don't know which way the adjective is facing. The whole thing is full of dangling, rotating, reversible qualifiers. And neologisms and obfuscations and tripe. It is inordinately concerned with physical and geographical description and the naming of ancestors. It lingers over complicated and tedious faux legalistic alliances, agreements, disputes and arbitrations. It leaps, both logically and chronologically, from one absurd set-up to another, painstakingly mapping out the ground upon which some action then briefly and violently takes place in a blur, without detail.

I quite like the rats.

It might, with a lot of work, make do as an overwrought piece of fantasy for teenage boys. But even then, a lot of the language would need taming. Or maybe not, I have no idea these days. But what Trainer is thinking of, handing the thing to me, I have no clue. His pitch is surely better suited to an editor half my age and with twice my cynicism. Someone who understands this kind of thing. Autism and body odour.

I skim the middle third. Remarkable overuse of 'cunt'.

Perhaps if it was rewritten as an urchin adventure. With the gangs calling themselves the wolves and the rats and the dogs etc. Estator himself could be the cripple king of the underworld. Where am I getting that from? I am remembering something. The humans would simply be adults. Perhaps that would work. Destitute children always work. Sentiment and holes in the clothes. Bands of brothers, clutching each other through the cold night. It would get rid of the tiresome genealogies accompanying each new character. All urchins come from the same place.

I take the final third and a Scotch to bed with me. It peters out in a feud with a man called Haft, chief ally of a crow called Whigs. It seems, at the end, unresolved, though Estator loses his brother, the handsome and swift Kona, ripped apart by a pack of dogs in, from what I can make out, a Homebase car park in Tottenham. They bury him, the Alliance Of The Moon, in the depths of Hampstead Heath, his body laid to rest on the rock of his ancestors in the Hollow Of The Third River, below the Hill Of Signs.

Jesus, as I say, Christ.

Well. I don't quite know what to think. Trainer is dead. Hung in his attic from a rafter. Though the police are *unhappy*, Morgan tells me excitedly from his noisy car. And have been in touch. They want a word. I may have been the last person he saw.

The drama.

I had always rather wanted that sort of death for myself. Though when it comes to it I'm much more likely to knock back a couple of dozen Percocet with a single malt chaser. Probably in Scotland. A rented house, or a hotel. Some terrible carpeting and cheap furniture and a print over the bed. *The Stag in the Glen*. Through the window a view of something or other. I should have been a father. Or a better person. Maybe I'll take my bottles up a mountain and find a sheltered overhang with a view of water and do it there. Last night I dreamed of someone very young, and I was his age, and he spoke to me kindly as if he liked me, and we walked by a river and nothing bad happened. Perhaps it was a memory. Though if it was it's not available to me while awake, thank goodness. I have succeeded in forgetting most people.

We've never had the police around before.

I take the bus and look out at the shops and think about Trainer. There'll be a funeral now, and I'll have to go. Morgan can drive. There's a wife, somewhere, I think. Children? I have no idea. Men like Trainer always seem to have short lives. He wasn't much younger than me I suppose. But featureless. Without landmark. Like a stretch of bland road between one town and another. Whereas I of course – I am all scenic route.

Estator climbs the trenches of Absalom's Gutter, reaching by dawn the edges of Whigs' Beakery in the full belly of Lumden Hammock. There is a side of hill there. Grass covers the lower third and makes a good retreat where a railway line once ran towards the glimmering. Anthos, son of Dresden, out of Dewden's cunt, roaming for thirteen moons in the low flooded plains of the north, adorned in stripes of his mounting fortune, climbed with Estator and took my flank to the Whigs's dark sided wheeling. They could see us but not align our purpose to the light. In short breaths we watched the day let blood. The cross ground gaps were clear to my eye, and I felt strength stored as bark in my limbs, and the scent of everything arranged itself and I detected Whigs himself in the dark interior of the wreck, his morning fetid body perched on the bones of my brother, and my brother still living in my heart and we the sons of Pohlner out of the cunt of Grip, my murdered brother, my heart. We attacked and brought down fourteen lesser flickers, Whigs himself escaping through sky with his cowardice squawking and Estator unwounded though Anthos lost an eye.

One of them is called Child. Would you believe it? I think of Byron. *Whilome in Albion's isle there dwelt a youth.* The other is almost called Harold, but not quite. Hardiman or something. They are terribly polite. And not ragged, not drab. I expected, I don't know why, something out of *The Sweeney.* But of course they're all smartly suited these days. Good shoes, shiny little phones, neat leather notebooks. *Spooks.* No . . . that's spooks, obviously. I can't think of any police dramas.

– And why did he want to see you?

– A book. He wanted to pitch a story at me.

He hesitates, the Child man. The other one looks at him.

– A story?

– A story, yes.

I wonder what the name leads him into. Bad jokes, of course. Wordplay. But do people make a metaphor of him? Or of themselves in front of him? Not that he would notice, in all likelihood, being inured.

– This was the first time you'd seen him? In a while?

– In about a year maybe. And not much before that. I used to . . . well I knew him when he was at Southern. Then there was drink, I heard, I believe. Though people are terrible talkers. As far as I know he's been doing freelance bits and pieces, and some ghost writing. That sort of thing.

– You were never particularly close then?

– No, no. Not at all. He's just been somebody, you know, in the business.

A telephone rings. It's the one who isn't Child. He shakes his head, retrieves it. Pokes a button.

– Sorry.

– So he had a story to tell you?

– To pitch to me. Yes. Yes he did. A silly fantasy thing.

– You weren't interested?

– Not my sort of bag at all I'm afraid.

– Can you say what it was about?

– A wolf. A band of wolves. And their adventures and conflicts with . . .

The policemen exchange a glance.

– . . . with various other groups. Foxes. Dogs. Ravens. What is it?

– Nothing. Please go on.

The one that isn't Child is writing furiously in his notebook.

– Well that was it really. Battles and so forth.

– He told you this?

– Yes. The outline of it.

– Did he show you a . . . er . . .

– Manuscript?

– Yes, was there a manuscript?

I travel as much as I can. I can afford it. I like hotel rooms. I like airports. I like train stations and large towns. I like cities. My French is good, my German passable. I travel alone. I enjoy art galleries. Museums, sometimes. I read for pleasure, for a change. I grow a beard, or I cut my hair very short. I hire prostitutes. Male or female doesn't matter. I like them to be thin.

– No. No manuscript. He described, merely. So . . . I can't remember the details.

– Had he actually written anything, did he say?

Oh they are very much at sea, these policemen. They both look at me. They look terribly trusting. I'm sure they aren't – not really. But they can look it. I wonder how skilled they are at managing their looks. Their expressions and their tone. I have spent a lot of time wondering what policemen will be like.

– I'm sorry. I haven't made myself clear. It was not *his* idea. It was not his story. He was presenting it to me on behalf of another. An author.

– Who?

Once, in Bucharest, I assaulted a boy. He was skinny and pale and he arrived with a black eye and I found him unco-operative and sullen and I hit him first and he laughed. I hit him again, a number of times. I kicked him. I threw a bathroom glass at him, and my toothbrush disappeared under the bed. I beat him with a bedside lamp. I hit him on the fucking head until he blacked out and then I cut his skin with broken glass and for a while I thought he was dead.

– I can't remember the name. Asian, I think. But no, I can't recall it.

– Ashid?

– Yes. Yes that was it. Ashid.

– You're sure.

– Positive. It was on the tip of my tongue.

– What did he tell you about Ashid?

– Nothing.

– Nothing at all?

– Nothing at all.

– There is a written version though. It's been written?

I roll that round my mouth for a moment.

– I believe so. Yes. Certainly, yes. There is a manuscript. And if I had been interested he would have brought it to me, I presume.

– He didn't have it with him?

– I don't think so. He would have shown it to me I'm sure, if he had. Wouldn't he? He would have got me to read the first couple of pages or something.

Child does a little shrug, a sigh. He is quite handsome. He considers me for a moment.

– The wolves, he says.

– Yes. The wolves.

– Did they have names?

– Oh. Goodness. Yes. There was one name. Certainly one name. The whole thing was a sort of memoir of this one wolf. Estragon? Escargot?

I laugh.

– Estator?

This is the other chap. He has something wrong with his face. Or perhaps it's just a bad shave. Sleep scars. Something or other. He looks somehow off kilter.

– Why, yes. I think so. Say it again?

– Estator.

– That's the one. How on earth did you know?

He ignores me and goes back to writing in his little book.

– It would be very helpful to us, says Child, if you could remember any more of the story. Names. And if there is anything else Trainer told you about the author. That would be particularly . . . well, it would be very helpful.

– I have to admit being immensely curious. You don't suspect foul play, do you?

They shrug, both of them, at precisely the same time, with exactly the same movement. It's quite comic. Child rubs an eye.

– No. Not as such. He didn't mention anything about expecting someone, or about having an appointment or anything, did he? Last night I mean, after he left you?

– No. Nothing like that.

– Have you ever been to his home? asks the non-Child.

– No.

– Did he mention that he'd been talking about this story to anyone else? Child again.

– No.

– Did he mention the name Gull?

The boy in Bucharest spat out a tooth and let them clean

him up and dress him and walk him out, all the time with his eyes on me, blank and empty, nothing in them, like painted-on eyes. I wish I had killed him. I am sure he is dead by now anyway. A life like that doesn't last. But still. It could have been me that ended it. But it was blown about instead by others – stepped on and kicked and thrown across rooms by dumb, ignorant others. Not by me. But I was afraid, in the hotel, that I would be caught.

– No.

– Price?

– Of what?

– No, I mean, the name . . . Price.

– No.

– Mishazzo?

– Me . . . ?

– Mishazzo?

– No, certainly not.

They finish up with the taking of phone numbers, the spelling of my address, with the exchange of cards. They tell me this and that. That they will be in touch again, that I am to call them at any time if anything comes back to me. That I am to report to them anything out of the ordinary. Especially any contact from anyone asking about Trainer, or about the manuscript. The *story*, Child calls it. I am to do my best to recall anything I might have forgotten. I am to try ever so hard.

I cannot recall the boy's name. Or how much I paid for

everything to be looked after. Or how much longer I stayed in Bucharest. Or whether it was before or after I killed the girl in Stockholm, or whether the girl in Stockholm had been as easy to kill as the girl in Glasgow whose throat I cut one Christmas Day and who seemed to me, in her confusion at the point of death, so useless, such an anti-climax.

Estator was still as the ground. The air was thick with the smell of man. Of his covered joints and his smoke. The slant of the earth mistook itself for a hill, but Estator was still as stone. He considered the brothers of the east and his sisters in the inner circle, and he counted to himself the generations leading to this point like the bough of a great tree. He spoke to the man.

— I will grant you the Lower Arches, Welland. You may store your metals there. You may come and go. You may not step into the Joiner's Wood. If you break this agreement I will kill your child.

— My Lord, said Welland. I am honoured and gratified. Blessings to your ancestors and your offspring and your days.

Estator sniffed him once more and felt no error nor change, and laid his forepaw on the ground in a gesture of peace, and turned with his escort of the blade, and travelled back to Smittenfield, by way of the Cross Gates, where new markings from men were investigated and found to be nothing but the putabouts of children.

*

What on earth are 'putabouts'?

If it's an allegory, it's one that I cannot decipher. But surely that's what it is. Full of references to gangsters, and cops-and-robbers codes. What else could it be, if the police are so keen, if they know the name of the lead character? What else?

I tell Morgan that I'm going to work at home in the afternoon, and he chases me with various bits and pieces until nearly two o'clock, but by three I'm at my desk looking out at the park and the air is cold and cluttered with patches of fog and cloud and people are in scarves.

It's some sort of exposé. It is a revelation of concealed things. It is secrets, laid out.

I pour myself a Highland Park and put my feet up and I keep a notepad by my side and I read the sweating manuscript again, and when I think I understand something I write it down. I do this for an hour.

Then I have a better idea.

The roads are scrapes on the ground and the buildings are scabs and the traffic is blood, and there the metaphor runs away from me somewhat. I spend most of my time getting rid of such things. Cutting and scoring through. I am all claw. And my thinking now is tangled.

I am on a bus full of children.

It has taken me a while, and the Internet, to work out the route. It's a two bus journey. The second of which has taken on board a troop of grey-and-black-dressed schoolkids.

They are all anoraks and backpacks and hand-held devices. They look, with their thermal hats and their earpieces, like commandos. Like paratroopers. As if this is a transport Chinook over night-time Helmand, and when the doors open they will GO, GO, GO, one at a time, plummeting fifteen thousand feet on to some high jagged plateau. Do they jump from that height? Probably not. But they are not silent and watchful, this crowd. There are no tight-eyed nerves and thoughts of home. That's their older brothers. This lot scream and shout and barge into people and are raucous to the point of frenzy.

I have never killed a child.

When you lift the skin from an arm or a leg it's very different to lifting the skin from the torso. And the back of the torso differs from the front. And on the front the abdomen differs from the chest, the shoulder from the pelvis, etc. The body is a multitude of ways of coming apart. I wonder about the differences with children. Scale. Finicky business, probably.

The bus rolls over little hills and down along narrow streets with the houses getting bigger and then smaller and then bigger again with economics. I sit tight. I listen to the children shouting. Sheer bloody murder. They smell of plastic and nylon. They are smeared in orange and Coke and crisp dust and stinking deodorants. They barge into each other. They are in the aisle beside me, pushing, calling, shouting, banging on windows for attention. I decide. I have decided. If one of them comes close, leans in to me, is pushed on to me, falls on to me, I will whisper in his or her ear. Calm and cold, so only she or he can hear:

Listen, right. If you touch me again I will cut your throat.

It will be the voice that scares them.

It's all railings and patches of balding grass, and damp mud and rubbish. There are no signs but for a small faded board, once blue, on which the ghosts of several business names can be made out. AXEL SYSTEMS. MASTERSONS. ALLISTON: SCRAP METAL. There is the vague smell of shit and diesel. I look at my shoes and the hem of my coat.

I walk past one way, going north I think, though the sun is nowhere to be seen and I really have no idea. It will be dark soon. It may be dark already. There is a wide gate, made of the railings – gunship grey – which is open, and inside I can see a portacabin thing on the right hand side, and a rough wall on the left, which seems to form part of a building. All grey brick, unpainted. There is a small ramp somewhere halfway down, clumsy concrete, and what may be a metal door. A door, anyway. Further on, I can't see.

I go as far as a corner. A lane runs down the side of the building, the railings pressed up against the grey bricks, their tops a three-pointed claw-like cutter leaning slightly out-wards, blunt and cold. The lane disappears into a drizzly distance, seeming to turn towards empty ground, wasteland. There is a clump of trees. Beyond there is either a railway or a road. Waste ground. Lost shoes. A jacket. Dusk, you'd call this, if you could see the sky.

I walk back the other way. It seems south only because the view has more in it. I can see some tower blocks in the middle distance, a huddle of office blocks to the right, where the bus left me. But I don't know where I am.

I look further in this time, and see a pile of car wrecks – shells – a muddy road, track really, turning to the right over puddles and reflections and shallow ruts of earth. A low open-fronted building with lights on, like a small warehouse, where I can see a man standing behind a van, his back to me, too far to make anything out. I walk as slowly as seems reasonable but still it isn't enough, and I can't make anything out to the right of the open building – though perhaps the curve of the track means that I wouldn't be able to anyway, I should have looked there first, too late now I'm past it. Just the railings now. Then a fence, a plain solid fence, and after a bit I can see the top of a shipping container. Or something very like a shipping container. Then the end of the fence. A dark building. Abandoned maybe.

There is the odd car passing on the road. The ones coming from the south surprise me each time as they crest the hump of the little bridge over what I hesitate to think of as a canal. Look at it. A ribbon of sick-looking tissue. Such as you get when you peel skin in strips from a bruised bit of back, for example. Looks liquid but barely is.

I go over the bridge. I stare at my phone. It's dark now,

more or less. There is a missed call from Morgan. I look at my shoes and the hem of my coat. I hesitate for a quarter of a minute. I think of Trainer hanging in his attic. It must be worth knowing – what makes a man do that.

I go into the little place. The enclosure. Like a camp. It is like a camp. Gypsies at the edge of town. I would not be surprised by a fire. There is no one around. The man who was at the van has disappeared. The van is where it was, but it's not Mastersons. *Axel Systems*, says a sign on a closed door. I'm not hiding. I'm just walking through here. Wide open. If anyone asks I will invent a car. Broken down, outside the town. No. That won't do it. A car though. I have a car that needs a new . . . wing. What sort of car? A Toyota. A Toyota Anus. Venus. There is mud everywhere.

I find what must be Mastersons. In a corner. Not what I thought of. It's a proper building. It looks old. Like it might at one point have been a roadside garage. A small hangar shape. Not so small maybe. Medium-sized. Lights on. There's a big M above the closed, wide, metal doors. A big old brown M. No life. Railings to the left. Wall to the right. You can see that the main hangar has some sort of extension there to the right. There is a small door set in to the big doors. On the right. A step-through. In the railings to the left there is an open gate. Seems to lead to the side of the building. There's noise. From inside. OK. So. Door in the doors to the right. Gate in the railings to the left. I stand in the mud looking up at the M.

Well what's the point of this?

I look down at my shoes. At the hem of my coat.

When you read some manuscripts they have no smell.

There's a car. A car coming. I can't . . . I dart through the gate, to the left. There are piles of things. Some barrels. Crates. I dart around one pile of things and behind another. I have no idea if I've been seen. What am I doing? Is this the exit? I have a car you see. A Toyota. Where is the man who knows about cars? Hello? Christ. Yes. Good day to you sir. Yes sir. No sir. Act like a moron. If you act like a moron they may think you're a moron. I turn. I'm hidden. There's the squelch of the tyres in the mud. A car. Stopped. Outside the railings. Exactly where I am. There's a radio. Radio music. I turn sideways. I have my back to the building. I'm behind a pile of crates. Slatted things. I can sort of see through them. A car door opens. Radio louder. Radio stops. Silence. Car door slams.

– Harry?

I can't tell if that's from inside or outside. Inside maybe. But loud. I look to the other side of me. There is an alcove. An inlet. What do you call it? A doorway. Shit. I dart past it. There is a stack of pallets. A low stack. I crouch behind it. I am now officially hiding.

Silence.

I think of a struggle in a Glasgow backstreet. She didn't like the walk to the rented car. It changed her mind. And something about me as well, doubtless. Messy, that. I had to leave her. She had rings. Little gold rings that kept their warmth on the shitty ground where her hand stretched out.

There's a rattling boom. It's the door. Fuck. Oh. No. Hold on. It's the other door. The door in the doors, the step-through at the front. At the front. I'm all right. I lean my head back. It's all dark up there now. In front of me is a tangle of bushes and nothing. He's gone in the other way. I hear a muffle of voices. Something dropped. Metallic. There are railings all around me. I'm in a sort of wide side passage. Against the long side there are the edges of next door's shacks and the weeds. Wooden shacks. Like old holiday camp chalets. Dark windows to my right. At the far end just the sweaty wood of old trees. Foliage and muck. I stand up slowly. I want to shit. I crouch again. What am I doing here? I feel stomach cramps, suddenly, and I think I'm going to have to shit. I really think I am. I am sweating. I fumble my hands beneath me. I press them to my backside. I press them against my hole, through my trousers. I cannot relax any muscle anywhere in my body or the shit will flood out of me. I try to concentrate on my breathing. My eyes rest on the space between two railings, ahead of me, straight in front of me. Two grey railings, black in the dark. But I know they are grey. Between them a patch of wood cabin. Jesus Christ. There is something glinting to my right. The light bouncing off a piece of silver paper or a fleck of paint. Ahead of me the rectangle of dark wood between railings, like an envelope. I try to think about an envelope. A white envelope, sealed. It helps. Christ.

Give me a minute.

I breathe. I would like a drink of water. My mouth is dry. I breathe. My heart is not thumping so much now, and I can hear the night start, and the murmur of voices behind me somewhere. Traffic in the distance. Trains. Whistles. Airplanes above me. I breathe. Two voices. Low. I stand up gingerly. I stop halfway. It all seems to be holding.

The doorway is deep set. It's dark. I can't see what sort of door it is. It's not a door. Is it? The thing is a sort of alcove, a muddy recess with some rubbish and a couple of . . . what? Paint cans. But the door . . . maybe it's covered up. It's a sheet of corrugated iron. Where there should be a door. I think about opening my phone and using its light to have a quick look. But I can hear the voices. It would be a stupid risk. I put my hands out ahead of me, as slow as possible, and I touch the side walls of the alcove. Brick. I take a step in. Immediately I take a step out again and look to my right. The car is parked outside the gate in the railings. I could probably, probably, sneak past it and away. I take a step in. I lean forward. I move my hands further. Still brick. I step again. I can touch the corrugated iron.

There's a sudden burst of laughter that seems terribly loud. I drop my hand. My body wants to move back, but I stay where I am.

Voices.

– Position, Harry. It's about position. And speed. You haven't got that sense of where you are then you haven't got anything, you know?

– What was that other guy's name?

– Who?

– The one with the hair.

I hear something behind me. Jesus.

I turn my head more suddenly than I should. The railings, and the envelopes of wood and the dark. I look down. A shape moves on the ground. I freeze. It's a cat. Is it? Yes. It's a fucking cat. It looks at me and its eyes are like drops of neon, and they turn away, and the cat wanders off. I am sweating again.

They're talking about a car now. Somehow. They have moved on. About an exhaust. They talk about a transmission. They talk about car things. I know nothing about cars. I glance back a couple of times but the cat is gone. I wonder if I should just leave.

– You hear anything?

I freeze.

– The wife was on again. She hasn't a clue.

– You sure?

– Course I'm sure. If she knew where he went or what's wrong with him she wouldn't be on the phone to me every fucking day crying her fucking eyes out.

– Not putting it on?

– Nah. No way. Not like that. Not with her tears. He spends all day in bed, she says. Is up all night, mostly sitting in the garden.

They're talking about Ashid's wife. Surely. Who else could they be talking about? So one of these men must be Palmer.

– I still think something happened to him. You know. Some sort of mental thing. It doesn't make any sort of sense otherwise. So solid for so long. Good bones. He has a lot to lose you know?

I am pressed up against corrugated iron. I think. I am trying to think. I am trying to remember the manuscript. *Good bones* means something. I remember wolves in the snow after midwinter, gathering by a stream to howl, in a ceremony, at the very edge of the city, the ceremony having something to do with marking the new edge of the city, the city expanding, and the ceremony is mournful and angry. Something moves to my left. By my feet. I turn my head. I look down. It's a rat. He sniffs. He seems to look at me. I am remarkably calm. Where is the cat? The rat seems to sit there. Considering. Behind him it is dark. Outside the doorway it is dark. Everything is dark. I move my foot, slightly, gently, just shifting the sole to the right. The rat moves. He lopes off out towards the railings.

– What's that?

– What?

I freeze.

– That thing.

– Oh. Piece from the Volvo what we had in Tuesday.

I don't know what to do now. I am sweating profusely. I decide I need to leave. I want to cough. It's sudden and irresistible. If I don't do something with it I will splutter. I cover my mouth. I crouch down and turn to my left. I worry about the rat. Or, I think that I should be worried about the rat, but in fact I don't care whether the rat is there or not. I cough. It is tiny. I know that it echoes in my head like a car crash and in fact it's nothing like as loud as that. As it seems. My throat relaxes. But I need water. I really do.

There's no talk. Silence. What are they doing? Are they likely to be armed? What does it matter? A wrench. A tyre iron. What is a tyre iron? There is clanging. Clanking. The first one is working still. The other one watching. I hope that is what is happening. I hope that they are not in fact moving slowly towards my hiding place, armed, carrying things. I stand up. My head spins a little and I see lights. One of them stays where it appeared.

It's a small hole. To my right. My eyes have adjusted to it. It is a rip in the iron, at the crest of a wave, the tip of one of the corrugations has been punctured, the hole's edges are a little frayed. If I put an eye to it will it look like an eye? I move a centimetre at a time to my right. I glance behind me. Nothing. I move some more.

– I was up at the sister's at the weekend.

I freeze.

– Oh yeah? How's she getting on then?

– She's good. You know. Good.

I move a little more. The hole is tiny. Smaller than a penny. A bullet hole? It's a bullet hole. I'm being stupid.

– Makes a change from the last place I'd say?

– What, Gibb's Court? Different world mate. Different

world. Kids don't know what's hit 'em.

– Oh yeah. How they like the new bloke?

I shift my head over the hole. I lean back from it. Slightly. I can't see a bloody thing. I lean forward. There are colours. Metallic surface. A gap. Some movement. I stop. I'm looking at the side of a car. Or a van. The two men are to the right somewhere.

– They're at that age, you know. Everyone is going to be, you know, viewed with suspicion. And he's a fucking estate agent. You know. He's all patter. They're not used to it are they? Sally's a quiet girl, always has been. So now they have this gobby bloke around all the time and I think if it was up to them, you know, on their own, they'd hate him.

I move my head closer. I can't see them. The car, or the van, is blue. It gleams. I can see nothing to the left. To the right there's this gap of light. They're there somewhere. Further than I'd thought. Movement. I pull back. Relax. There's movement. I don't know what that is. An arm. A leg.

– But they have this thing for their mum, you know. Fierce loyal. Thick as thieves, the three of 'em. They want her happy. They're protective. And he's all right really. He's no dope. He's doing it right. You have to be honest, you know. Kids are smart. They'd spot the bullshit before their mother would.

You smell bullshit. You don't spot it. You could I suppose. My nose touches the iron. It's cold. It makes me jump. Not externally. Internally. Where I am. I'm seeing more blue. I imagine overalls. Blue overalls. I have no idea. Movement. In the gleam. In the blue of the van. Car. Van, I think. A reflection. I'm seeing a reflection of a movement. He's, one of them, working on something. On another car. Van. A different one.

– So they put up with him. And he's no fool. He's not trying to win them over, you know. No taking them on trips or buying them presents or any of that. He's taking his time.

– You've warmed to him.

– Have I?

– You hated him.

– I didn't hate him. I just wasn't sure. She's my sister, you know. What she's been through. I was . . .

– Alert.

– Alert, yeah.

He laughed.

– I was alert, all right.

I am learning nothing. This banal banter seems so completely unconnected to anything I know about that I wonder if it's coded. Why would it be coded, you idiot? They've just drifted off into life. Nothing about Trainer. Not even a mention. Nothing to suggest they even know about Trainer. I take a step back. I account for all of my limbs, and I gently turn around.

The rat and the cat are sitting by the railings, looking at me.

I swear to God.

Suddenly my nose is running and I think it's blood.

Can't be blood. Why would it be blood?

They're just sitting there, side by side, two cartoon silhou-
ettes. The rat and the cat. Deep black against the grey railings
and the envelopes of wood, their eyes like four bright ghosts
– two small ones on the left, two slightly larger higher up on
the right.

– You done?

I freeze. I'm already frozen. Nothing moves. Behind me
there's more clanging. The sound of a sliding door sliding
shut, as on a van. There is the clanking of tools dropped in a
toolbox. A cleared throat.

– That for Gull?

– Yeah.

Nothing else. They say nothing else. Gull. At least I heard
Gull. Something for Gull. A package. Money perhaps. Drugs.
The four eyes look at me. They don't blink. They don't move.
Maybe they're not eyes. What am I looking at? They are eyes.

Banging behind me.

Clanging.

Banging.

Lights go out somewhere.

The rat moves. He ducks his head. Sniffs the ground. His
eyes swoop down and disappear. I see him moving. His body
moving. The cat just sits there. I swear to God. Looking at me.
Now the cat looks at the rat. Everything I see is a sludge of
dark and darker patterns, shapes, movements. I might as well
be in oil, underwater. The slightest shift of my gaze alters

everything, so the rat is there, then there, and the cat is over there, or moved now, over there.

I hear the voices to my left. Quieter. Further away. More outside than inside. I hear the big doors, the metal doors, the double doors.

The cat looks back at me. The rat is at my feet. The rat is sniffing my feet. My shoes.

A slam. Slam. I jump. The rat jumps, runs off. Runs back to the cat. The door in the doors. The step-through. I hear fiddling with locks now. Chains.

Then. This. Noise close to me. Still on my left. Gate. The gate. The gate in the railings. It's slammed shut. Shit. More chains, locks, keys. They're locking the gate. They're locking me in. The rat is beside the cat again. The cat hasn't moved. Well they don't, do they? I could step out. Hello. Crikey, how embarrassing. Could you just let me . . . ? No? No. They're at the car already. One of them is. Now there is a high-pitched squeaking, regular. The cat and the rat seem to stiffen. I look at them. They are painted black. Their eyes are buds. It's the alarm. They're putting on some sort of alarm. Damn it. There is one long beep to finish. Then a pause. Another car door opens. What if there are sensors? Movement sensors? Lights that come on? A car door slams. Another one closes. The engine starts up. The rat suddenly scampers off, as if to see them go. If there is a light . . . I press back into the doorway. The cat disappears. Its eyes go out. It's not there. No light. The car rumbles, turning, and is louder for an instant, and then it quickly fades and a silence comes up out of the dark black ground where I cannot see my feet.

I want to blow my nose. I run my hand over it, and my hand is wet, with either snot or blood. Snot, obviously. I take a step. It will be like this for a while. I want to shit.

Traffic in the distance. Tyres. I think I can hear them go over that little bridge. That lovely little bridge. I can't see any bloody cat, or rat. I look at the sky and it isn't there. Everything is dark. The grey railings stutter through the black like tracks, and I follow them, my feet finding mud and pools and soft accumulations of God only knows, and getting out will make a mess of me, I know it. They will have such a puzzle, Child and his partner, if I die here, impaled on the triangular tops of the railings, my neck broken, my face chewed off. I shudder and swallow and look for a handkerchief. There's a tissue in my coat pocket. I wipe and look at it and I can see nothing. The white of it seems just as blurred and grey as when I started. There is a light ahead of me somewhere, in the centre of the compound. Yes, compound is about right. Are there dogs? Jesus.

I miss you.

The gate is chained, padlocked. The railings are high. This gate. To the side of this building. Which is now alarmed. Which has a rat. If I get out of this I will still have to get out of the compound proper. The whole thing. Maybe . . .

I look behind me. The other end of this enclosure borders on the world. Only one set of railings. Then what? What is there? Waste ground. Brambles and trees. The rat. The rat and his brothers. The wolves. The wolves and their voices. Their eyes in the dark. I want to laugh. On the ground at my feet there is a tin can that's been stamped on. A 7UP can. The dent has raised points in the aluminium. The light glints off them. Like eyes. I look back at where the cat was. There is nothing there now. The railings run into the darkness. Behind them on the left the dark wood of the cabin next door, like a prison camp. At the end, through the grey rack, is just blackness and bright dots like gaps or non-gaps, like absences, presences, and rustling and movement that could be there, or here in my head, which is where I am whatever I do and which appears to me now – look at it! – a fetid dark place full of shit.

I have never killed anyone in my life.

The water closed over the sun and the moon and Estator stretched his neck and the gathered host howled and raked the dark earth and proclaimed the King Of The Wolves. His first-born son rolled in the leaves and Klew scratched the name of the new King into the Tree Of The Hidden Tree. The hawks in the night carried tribute. Dogs from the western mansions bowed seriously. The company of Pauper Rats giggled in the shallows and the ravens of Clerkenwell screeched in the branches of the surrounding woods like human young. Estator breathed deeply and knew that all these creatures soon would be blood and decay and the soil, and that the soil was his food, and that he himself would not live as long as his name or his deeds, and that all he now did was done forever, because it would be spoken of and told, and he was no longer himself but a story. He looked at the fox companions, and they smiled at him, and he was filled with sorrow at the closing down of his life. At the closing down of his life.

There were no dogs. No guards. No wolves.

I think my finger is broken.

My coat is torn in three places. It is smeared in mud and at least two different sorts of shit. My shoes are caked and scratched, and there are pebbles and gum and a bottle cap stuck to the heels.

On the bus a woman sat beside me and then moved.

There is a small cut on my forehead, and a rather larger one on my left cheek. I stand in the bathroom watching myself in the mirror as I take off my clothes. There is considerable bruising to my chest. There is a scrape across my back, which curls around my hip and plunges into my groin. The are patches of dirt in impossible places. And a surprising gash on my thigh with no corresponding tear in my trousers that I can see.

The chief sources of pain are my finger – the ring finger of my left hand – and my ankle, my right ankle, which is swollen. It's a sprain I think. I went over on it when I landed – immediately after injuring my finger by almost leaving it behind, trapped between the spurs on the top of the fence.

I can see no reason for anything. Certainly not for any of this.

Trainer must have had exposed beams in his ceiling. Or a hook, or something like that.

Sitting on the bus all the liquids running out of me started to dry, and I was unsure which trickle was blood, and which was sweat, and whether I had pissed or shit myself. There is less to it than I felt there was and I am disappointed.

I hate my life.

I read stories all day long. All week long. I read them. I hear them. I listen to stories and plots and fictions. I weigh characters in my hand like I am buying fruit. I purse my lips and roll my head on my shoulders and I suggest this and that. It might make more sense if you did this. It would be more believable, the character would be more sympathetic, the story would flow better, the loose ends would be tied up if you did this or that or the other. And they do it. And people read these things. People actually read them from within their lives and the pages are numbered and the numbers are sequential.

No one saw me there. I was not apprehended.

Time stretches but it never breaks. It never breaks.

There are no beams or hooks or anything likely in my flat. There is rope. I have rope. Unused rope. It lies on top of my wardrobe neatly tied in a pinched loop. I have never been this angry before. I have never been this furious or cold.

I pour a Highland Park. I think about Trainer. I wonder about him. What a terrible mess he made of his life. I consider that judgement and I look out at the park. Naked, I sit in my armchair and I stare out at the mist over the grass and the cold light in the trees and the crisp shadows where things move and sway and inch forward and retreat.

Knowing things completes them. Kills them. They fade away, decided and over and forgotten. Not knowing sustains us. Why do I care about Trainer? I do not. Why do I care about a worthless manuscript that smells of contrivance? I do not. All I am doing is comparing my own set of misunderstandings to the misunderstandings of others. All I am doing is wishing that I were not what I am. All I am doing is constructing a story that might be told about me when I have given up hearing the stories of others.

I am naked. I can dress. I can dress and go downstairs. I can take the manuscript with me. I can cross to the park.

The night is bitter and dark. The air is empty. I dig with my hands in the hard earth beside a high tree in sight of my windows. My finger runs pain through me like a hot iron. I make a shallow depression and I put the manuscript there and I cover it up with dirt and I make no great effort to disguise it. I limp back across the road. I pick up a rock. I fling it at my window, my office window, and it punches a hole through a pane and lands on my desk. I struggle back upstairs. I leave my door open. I pull over bookcases, tables, I knock pictures from walls. I smash a vase, I break bottles, I throw the contents of cupboards and drawers on the floor. I pull books apart, I rip covers from them, I kick a crack in the television screen, I dial Child's number and when he answers I throw the phone against the wall and roar. I find it again and pick it up and plead with him to come, to come now, and then I roar again and drop the phone on the kitchen floor and stamp on it. I turn over my own bed. I open the fridge, pull out the shelves, pull it over. I smear my blood on the walls. I turn on a gas ring, light it, turn it to full. I strip. I tear my clothes. I get the rope from the top of my wardrobe. I tie one end around my neck. I tie the other end around the . . . what?

All of this I can do. I can do it. Child and non-Child. Pages to turn. I will become fascinating to them. Never ending.

I sit in my armchair. Naked.

I can do it. I will do it.

I sit in my armchair.

Naked.

What to tie the rope to, though. That's the bloody problem, isn't it?

Rothko Eggs

She liked art. She liked paintings and video art and photography. She liked to read about artists and she liked to hear them talk. She had been to all the big London art museums already, and she had been to some small ones too, and some galleries. She wanted to be an artist, she thought. She liked the way the world looked and felt one way when you looked at it or breathed or walked about, and looked another way completely when you looked at art, even though you recognized that the art was about the world, or had something to do with the world – the world you looked at or breathed or walked about in. She didn't mean realism. She didn't like realism very much really, because usually there was no room in it. She would look at it, and everything was already there. But she liked abstract art because it was empty. Sometimes it was only empty a tiny amount, and it was easy for her to see what the artist was trying to say or make her feel, and sometimes that was OK, but she usually liked the art that had lots of empty in it, where it was really hard to work out what the artist wanted, or whether the artist wanted anything at all, or was just, you know, trying to look like he had amazing ideas.

But really good artists had lots of empty in their paintings or whatever they did. They left everything out, or most things anyway, but suggested something, so that she could take her own things into the painting (or the installation or the video or whatever) and the best art of all was when she didn't really know what she was taking in with her, but it felt right, and when she looked at that art and took herself into it she felt amazing.

She wanted to be able to do that. Make that.

Photography was a bit different. She hadn't worked out why yet.

Her dad was having a text fit. She put her phone on silent and stuck it in a drawer.

She was trying to finish her history essay but Beth kept on popping up on MSN asking her stupid questions. She didn't answer her for a while and then set her status to away and tried to think about why Churchill lost the election after the war.

There were some artists that she couldn't really understand. She could see that they had left her lots of space, but she didn't know what to fill it with. Sometimes, if they were not very well known or respected artists she decided that they just weren't very good – that they were faking it and they didn't know what they were doing really. But if they were famous and supposed to be amazing then they just made her feel stupid. It was easier the further back in history you went, because art became more realist and you could just like something or not like it. More or less. Though sometimes when you didn't like something and then read about it, or read about the artist, you could start to see things you didn't notice before, or you could feel things differently, and start to like it. Unless you went back to when everything was sort of cartoonish, like Fra Angelico, and then she didn't really understand what was going on there either, because it just looked so sloppy and bad. But apparently it was amazing.

On her laptop the wallpaper was a self portrait by Frida Kahlo. She liked it. She thought it was sort of funny, because it looked so serious. She liked this woman. She had seen a film about her. That wasn't why she liked her though. She liked the way she made people fit her world, and be a bit ugly, but still make them beautiful. And funny. There were not enough women artists in history. She paid them extra attention when she came across them. She wondered if that was fair, and then wondered why she wondered that. It was not a competition. She was not a judge. So she decided she could pay them more attention if she wanted.

On her wall she had some small postcards lined up in a grid. There were quite a few now. It was useless to look at any one of them really, because the prints were so small, and you could get only the vaguest sort of idea of what they were really like. She had seen some of them for real. But there were thirty-eight now, in seven rows of five, and one row of three at the top. Two more and then she'd start another grid. Her dad had sent most of them. Or just given them to her. But there were ones from her gran as well, and from friends, and her mother had picked up a few when she'd gone to the National Gallery in Edinburgh on her weekend away. She suspected her mother had just gone into the shop.

The grid was really neatly spaced and aligned. She didn't like that now. She wished it was more disorganized. She'd made it look like a chart. But she'd decided to leave it as it was and make the next one messy in contrast. She thought that would be interesting. It had started by accident, when she just stuck her first postcard – of the Thames, by Turner – on the wall above her desk. It was only when she'd added the third that she lined them up properly. And then she told people she liked art postcards. So more came. She'd only been doing it about a year. She wondered how long it would take to fill all the empty space on all the walls.

She had a Francis Bacon exhibition poster that her dad had bought for her. She had a really nice print of a young Rembrandt self-portrait where he looked mad and sort of handsome. She also had a poster of Van Gogh's *Starry Night*, which she hated, but which she had to leave there, at least for now, because her mother had bought it for her. She didn't hate it. But it was so clichéd that she couldn't help deciding not to like it. Her favourite print was the one over her bed. It was *Judith Slaying Holofernes* by Artemisia Gentileschi. Her mother didn't like it at all. She said it would give her nightmares. All that blood. But it didn't. It was really violent, but it was like that wasn't the point. The point was something else. It was the way Judith gritted her teeth. It was good.

Her mother was calling her. She shouted back. She opened the drawer and looked at her phone. OK. No new texts from her dad. She read the last one. He was panicking about the summer holidays. It wasn't even Easter yet. If they talked to each other and left her out of it everything would be sorted in about ten seconds. She hated clichés. Except maybe it would be a cliché if they got on really well and were all mature all the time and made sure she never felt like a football or whatever, and were super civilized and cool. That would be another cliché. At least it would be a more pleasant cliché. Maybe it wouldn't. Maybe it wouldn't because it would feel forced and unnatural, whereas at least this was them being honest.

– Is he annoying you?

– What?

Her mother was in the doorway.

– Your father.

– No. Why?

– You're sighing at your phone. You always sigh at your phone when he's texting you.

– I don't. It's not him. It's Michele.

– Why are you sighing at Michele?

– Oh, she thinks she's pregnant. Again.

Her mother stared at her for a second. And relaxed.

– Jesus, Cath, don't do that. It's not funny. I am . . . God almighty. Just don't.

She smiled. Her mother stuck out a hand.

– Washing.

– No, I put it all in the basket.

– What's that then?

There was a pair of socks on the bed.

– They're clean. They're today's.

– All right. Come down for a cuppa.

– I will in a minute. I'm doing an essay.

– Well I'm putting the kettle on. Come down and have a cuppa with me. I'm bored. Do you want to go to the shops?

– No. I'll be down in a minute.

She waited until she was alone again and then replied to her father. *Yes. No. I did. There is. It will be all right. Shut up.* She knew that if something terrible happened to her, her parents would have to meet in casualty or the morgue or something and they would break down and cry and hug each other and all the dumb fighting would be forgotten and they would love each other again, because she was dead or a vegetable and that was all they had. And then she imagined herself thinking that if she really loved them she'd kill herself and she laughed. Then she thought that if something terrible happened they would blame each other and spend the rest of their lives tied together by hatred and her death.

Everything was a cliché.

Sometimes when she was out with her dad and they were talking with other people, he would refer to her mum as 'my ex-wife'. One day she asked him if he ever referred to her as his ex-daughter. They had a row. But since then he referred to her mum as 'Catherine's mother'. Which made it sound like her fault.

Churchill lost the post-war election because people were tired. When you have a fire in your house you want the fire brigade to come. When the fire is out you want them to leave. She wrote this in her essay and was really pleased with it. She thought it was a brilliant analogy. But when she got it back she'd been given 56% and there were no comments at all, and the bit where she said that wasn't even ticked or marked. She didn't know why she bothered.

He waited for her sometimes in a coffee shop near her school. She'd get a text at exactly 3.30 saying 'fancy a quick coffee?' even though she never actually had a coffee, she had one of their herbal teas, or sometimes a smoothie. Sometimes she couldn't meet him because she had something on, or was going somewhere with Beth or Michele. Sometimes she pretended she had something on. Well, just once or twice. Usually it was fun to see him. He was usually in a good mood. He'd tell her funny things about work. About people at work or people he'd met. He'd tell her about gangsters. Ridiculous cartoon gangsters with stupid names – and it always took her ages to realize that he was making them up. Sometimes he'd get a call and have to leave in a hurry. She liked that. He'd say *What* into his phone and then listen and grunt or say *yes* or *no*, and then he'd sigh and say *all right ten minutes*, and he'd stand up and kiss her on the forehead and whisper that he loved her and he'd be gone.

The coffee shop was at a crossroads. She had to walk past it on the way home. Down the road from the school. Then the zebra crossing. One time she was walking past it and she glanced in and her dad was sitting there. He hadn't seen her. He was reading a newspaper. She just looked at him. She was with a couple of people. Stuart and Byron and Felice. Or something. So she couldn't really just stop. But she lingered. And looked at him. He was reading. Every so often he'd look up. But he was looking out towards the crossing. He'd missed her. He looked worried. He looked sad and worried and tired. He looked the way he always looked when he didn't know she could see him. Then when he saw her he'd light up. Or – well, not light up, but his face changed. He would smile. And yeah, he'd brighten up a little. And she liked that. But his face when she wasn't in front of him worried her. He sat slumped. He looked old. Older. Did he fake it when he saw her? Or did seeing her just make him happier than he really was? She didn't like it either way. She caught up with the others. Later she got the text that he must have sent at 3.30. It had been lost somewhere. She replied immediately and he texted back saying it didn't matter, it was no big deal, he'd just been passing. Love.

*

She and Stuart had sort-of-sex in his bedroom one Saturday afternoon. Everyone thought he was gay, and he never really cared one way or the other about that and never denied it or got angry or anything, so she had thought he was gay too. And he liked books and art, so . . . and he wore a scarf in a sort of gay way, and he was good friends with Byron, who was actually gay. But it turned out he wasn't gay. Or wasn't very gay anyway. He was a really good kisser. Kissing him was . . . really good. She talked to Beth about it, and she had wanted to describe what the kissing was like; and she wanted to tell her that kissing Stuart was *like being inside a Jackson Pollock painting.* She really wanted to say that. She was determined to say that. But when it came to it she just said that it was *really good,* and *bare sexy.* It made her think that maybe Beth and her weren't as close as she thought. Because why else would she not say what she wanted to say? It was just stupid.

Stuart talked to her about art. She knew more than he did. He seemed interested in listening to her. He sent her an email saying he'd looked up Francis Bacon online and thought he was mad and brilliant. But she thought he was faking it a bit. And it was the first she'd heard from him since the sort-of-sex, and he didn't mention that at all, or her really either, or mention anything about meeting up again outside school or whatever. He had film posters on his wall. *Watchmen* and *Superbad,* and an old *Finding Nemo* one that she thought was cute but which made him blush when she mentioned it.

When he took off his jeans she saw a big scar on his leg.

Just above his knee, on the back of his leg. She wanted to know what it was, but she didn't ask.

She read about horrible things in the newspapers. She read about fathers who killed their kids because they hated their ex-wives. They strangled them or poisoned them or drove them off a cliff. She read that stuff all the time. Just when she had forgotten about one case, a new one would turn up. Or she'd hear about them on the TV or the radio. Her mother always went dead quiet when stuff like that came on. And sometimes she'd mutter something. Something like *the poor things*, or *what a bastard*. And Cath would think about her father. About him slouched over his coffee without her. She could scare herself for a short while thinking like that. But not for very long. Her father was very gentle. Very kind. He had never smacked her, even when she was little and screamed all the time. Her mother had smacked her. He'd never even shouted at her. Or not that she could remember. Or not in a way that made her remember. He was always gentle. He would say nothing, just open his arms, and she would lie against him and he would wrap her up and she would stay like that for ages. That was when she was little. They hadn't done that in a long time. But she would do that again without even thinking.

She wanted to ask him whether he had ever had a case like that. A father who kills his kids. Or anything like that. But he never told her any of the bad stuff. She knew he had to investigate all sort of things – murders and everything. She'd seen him on the news once. The London news. Detective Inspector Mark Rivers. It was weird, seeing his name like that. And him asking for witnesses after a boy was stabbed somewhere. He'd been really good. He talked about the boy like he'd known him, about his family and stuff. It was all good – the way people are after they're dead. It had made her nearly cry, because she was proud of him she supposed. But he only ever told her about the funny stuff. Or he made it up.

– No, Dad, that's Pollock.

– Watch your language.

She laughed.

– Pollock. Jackson Pollock. He does the ones with the paint all over the place all scrambled and splattered and stuff.

– Do you like them?

– Yeah.

– Not so much though?

– Well, I like them. They're fun. I'd like to see them for real, because the paint is meant to be really thick and that would be amazing to see them up close. But they're like . . .

– A mess.

– No. They're like the idea of having an idea, instead of having an idea.

She laughed at herself. Her Dad made an *ooh* noise. They turned a corner.

– Is that art teacher of yours any good?

– Yeah, she's OK.

– Are you smarter than her?

She laughed, thinking *yes!*

– No.

– Have you told her you want to go to art college?

– I don't know if I want to go to art college.

– Oh. I thought you did.

– Well I want to do art, but I don't know if I want to go to art college or do art history. First.

– First?

– Maybe.

– Well. No hurry.

He pulled in to the kerb in front of the house. She leaned across and kissed him. She knew he wanted a hug. But it was awkward, hugging in the car, and she didn't like it.

– Will you call me during the week?

– Yes.

– How's your mother?

He always left it to the last minute. So that she could only say

– She's fine.

– OK. I love you.

– I love you too.

– Speak soon.

He waited for her to get to the front door. As if something might happen to her between the car and the house. Then when she put her key in the lock he drove off, as if nothing could happen to her then until the next time.

*

She liked Tracey Emin, even though everyone else she knew didn't like her, and some people seemed to hate her. She liked her voice best of all, and she loved to hear her talk. She saw her once, walking through Smithfield Market looking really hung over. She'd wanted to talk to her, but she'd been too shy, and her friend Michele didn't know who she was and there was no one else to be excited with. She didn't like Damien Hirst at all. She thought he was an idiot. And his work was ugly and full of boyish things, like he was a permanently horny boy trying to get some, and everyone was just embarrassed to have him around. She thought Sarah Lucas was like that too. But she didn't say it. She just said that Lucas didn't really move her. It was a way she had of dismissing something without sounding judgemental. She had learned it from a documentary about Francis Bacon. She couldn't remember now whether it was Bacon who said it about some other artist, with a smirk on his face, or whether it was someone else who'd said it about Bacon. She liked Jake and Dinos Chapman. She liked the way they could make her feel a bit sick, but that she kept on peering at their models and their pictures anyway because all the detail had something in it that was important but it kept on shifting somewhere else, like when you have a floater in your eye. She liked Grayson Perry. She liked his voice too, and she liked hearing him talk about art, and she had some podcasts of a radio show he'd done. But she didn't really know his art. She liked the way he shocked her mother whenever he turned up on the telly in one of his mad frocks. She'd been to the Turner Prize exhibition for the last three years. She had liked Zarina Bhimji most in 2007. In 2008 her favourite was either the photographer, or Goshka Macuga's wooden things like people trees. In 2009 she hadn't really liked any of them. They didn't move her.

On the Tuesday after the Saturday when they'd had sort-of-sex and Stuart had sent her an email about Bacon, and a couple of texts about nothing, he came up to her in a corridor in school and, blushing very red, asked her did she want to go for a coffee after school, just the two of them. She didn't know why he was blushing. Well, she did, and she thought it was funny, but it made her blush as well. The two of them just standing there going red. She rushed out a *Yeah, OK, see you after*, as casually as she could and walked off. It was completely stupid. They'd had about six million conversations in the school corridors before.

One time in the café two men came in and sort of stood there looking at her dad. He stared back at them.

– What.

It was the same voice he used on the phone.

– Sorry to interrupt, sir.

The one talking was a really good-looking black man with dark framed glasses and hair shaved close to his head. He was wearing a dark grey suit, with a black v-neck jumper under the jacket and his tie done up. He looked really interesting. The other one was a white guy with a funny face. Like he was peeking through a keyhole. Or maybe it was normal. He had a stupid smile and was carrying a big envelope and he was looking at her. He was wearing a neat suit too, but he looked more like he was going for a job interview. They didn't look like police.

– What.

– Need you to have a look at a couple of things, the black one said. Somewhat urgent.

He pushed his glasses up his nose and looked at Cath and nodded.

– I'm very sorry to bother you.

She smiled and felt herself blush.

Her dad went outside with them. She watched through the window. The three of them hunched over the envelope, and stuff was pulled out of it, and her dad peered at it. She thought maybe it was photographs. She couldn't see. Her dad made a call on his phone. The black guy made one on his. The white guy came back in and bought himself a bottle of water.

– Sorry about this, he said.

– That's OK.

– He'll be back in a minute.

He seemed nice. But he looked sad. She thought that he just had one of those sad faces. And red eyes. She wanted to ask him things. About her dad. What's he like to work with? Is he tough? Does he beat people up? Is he racist? Does he swear

169

all the time? Is he good at being a detective? Is he clever? Is he sexist? Does he have a girlfriend? Do you do cases where fathers kill their kids? What does he think about them? But she couldn't form any sort of question at all before he had gone back outside. The two men walked to a car and drove away and her father came back in and patted her shoulder and apologized.

– That's the first time I've ever met anyone you work with.

– No it's not. Is it?

– Yeah. You're very rude to them.

He laughed.

– I am not.

– You didn't say anything to them. Just *what*. You should have asked them to sit down.

– They should have called me.

– They seemed really nice. You should have introduced me.

He smiled at her as he sipped his coffee.

– They are not nice. Really. And anyway, one of them is married and the other is gay and they're both old enough to be your father. And if your mother and I agree on anything then we agree that you should never, ever, ever, get involved with a policeman.

They went up towards Muswell Hill to a place Stuart knew where there'd be no one from the school. He bought her a strawberry tea and got himself a cappuccino. He talked about music and kept on wiping his lips. He was into all these bands that she had never heard of. She thought he was trying to match her art talk. Trying to balance it. That was OK. He said he'd send her a playlist and they talked for a while about the best ways of sharing files, and about the computers they had and about stuff on Facebook, and she was sure they'd had all these conversation a dozen times before. It was like he'd forgotten that he'd known her for about two years. On and off.

They walked down the hill and he held her hand for a while. When they got to a bus stop that was good for her, he kissed her again, and it was great. He leaned against her and she could feel his body warm against her and she liked it and she thought about his scar. When the bus came he smiled at her like he was shy again, and she liked that too, and he said 'See ya, gorgeous' in a stupid voice and they both laughed, and they were laughing at themselves, at how stupid they were being and that it was all right to be stupid, it was fun. On the bus she dozed and held her phone in her hand and leaned her head against the window.

She didn't know what to do about Rothko. She didn't understand Rothko. Everything about Rothko made her want to like him. All the things people who liked him said and wrote made her want to like him. They talked about warmth and love and comfort and feelings like religious feelings. She wondered about herself, about what was wrong with her that she couldn't feel those things. Or not feel them when she looked at Rothko. She had been, twice, to the Rothko room in the Tate. And her dad had taken her to the big exhibition of lots of his stuff. But she didn't get it. Soft focus blocks of dusty colour. One of them had made her think of sunsets on summer holidays in Cornwall, so she liked that one, a bit. But Rothko. He did not move her.

Whenever her father took her to one of the Tates, or to the National Gallery or something, she could sense his boredom make his back straighten and his eyes water. She would forget he was there sometimes and then turn to find him looking at his phone, or looking at a woman, or yawning. She'd laugh at him and they'd go for a coffee and he'd get her something in the shop. Some postcards usually, or a book. She didn't like him spending much. She didn't know why. He wasn't hard up.

Her mother was jealous of these trips. She didn't want to be, and she battled with herself to cover it up, but you could feel it, in the kitchen. It was like she was plugged in to something.

She started going to museums and galleries with Stuart. They went to the Whitechapel Gallery together – the first time she'd been. They had to stand on the tube and he held her hand. She liked when they had to let go for some reason and then she'd wait to see how long it took him to reach out for her again. Sometimes it wasn't quick enough and she grabbed his hand, and she liked that she felt able to do that, and liked that it made him smile. She liked the fact that they were turning into a really annoying couple who held hands all the time and that their other friends, if they knew, would dedicate their lives to taking the piss.

They went to the National Gallery and spent a couple of hours wandering around. Stuart wasn't scared of stuff that other boys were scared of. He stood in front of a picture of a naked man and said out loud to her that it was beautiful. He looked at another picture and wanted her to tell him whether it was supposed to suggest a vagina. She blushed and he didn't. When she used a word he didn't understand, he told her he didn't understand it and asked her what it meant. She had to admit once that she didn't really know what crescendo meant. He laughed at her and put his arm around her shoulder and gave her a little kiss on her cheek.

She told her mother that she and Stuart were sort-of-seeing-each-other now. Her mother took a couple of minutes to work out which of her friends she meant. Then she told her that he was welcome to come over to the house whenever Cath wanted. That made her laugh. She liked it. She wondered if he'd be allowed to stay the night. Maybe. In the spare room. She wondered if he'd even want to. She wanted him to. Sometime. For some reason. She wanted to see him first thing in the morning. She imagined bringing him a cup of tea in bed. She imagined him lying asleep in the spare bed in the spare room. She imagined it for ages.

*

Her dad was obsessing now about the crossing outside the café, near the school.

– Some kid is going to get run over one of these days.

– Why?

– 'Cos you lot never look. You just walk across. And cars come up that road too fast. There should be traffic lights. Not just a crossing.

She looked. Most of the younger kids were gone by now. There were a few people she recognized outside the shop on the other side. She'd never seen anyone even come close to getting run over.

– You should be careful.

She laughed.

– Don't laugh. I worry about things like that. They may seem stupid to you but there you have it. I can't help it, I'm your father.

He was in a mood.

– You need to be careful. The number of teenagers killed on the road in London is horrific. You know? Never mind knife crime and drugs and all the stuff you get warned about all the time. Well, do mind them, but you know about that stuff. It's the traffic you might just forget about. Forget to look out for. You're to be careful about that.

A group of uniforms passed the window. She looked up and saw Byron, who gave her a wave. And Stuart's head appeared from behind him, smiling at her. Her dad looked.

– Your friends?

They walked on. Stuart looked back, still smiling. She found herself smiling and blushing.

– How's the flat, she asked, to cover it.

– Do you have a boyfriend?

– Oh Dad.

He was smiling at her. She was so obvious. She was a cliché. Her cheeks burned.

– Which one? The black boy?

He was turned around in his chair now, looking after them. Stuart noticed and looked away, and then they disappeared.

– The one who looked back?

– They're just friends.

– So why are you blushing like a berry?

She laughed.

– Like a berry?

– Like a strawberry.

– People don't blush like berries.

– Which one was he then? What's his name?

So she told him a bit about Stuart. But nothing like as much as she'd told her mother. He smiled at her and nodded but she could tell he was sad. Because she was growing up and all that clichéd crap.

She imagined walking from school one day and hearing a bang and a scream, and another scream, and seeing something happening at the crossing. She imagined running up, and as she got closer her friends trying to hold her back. She imagined seeing Stuart lying on the ground, pale, a trickle of blood coming out of his mouth. She imagined kneeling beside him and holding his head, and looking into his eyes and him looking at her with the most intense eyes that she had ever seen, and dying. She imagined a girl screaming and sobbing, and Byron crying and holding her hand, and she imagined her dad arriving with the two men from the coffee shop, and her dad helping her up and moving her away, and the good-looking black man and the other one trying to restart Stuart's heart, and the black guy looking up at her dad and shaking his head, and Stuart being beautiful.

Then she imagined that she was the one hit by a car, and Stuart was holding her, tears running down his face. She preferred the idea of him dying. She laughed and wondered whether she could tell him about all this and knew that of course she couldn't.

She told Byron that she'd met a gay cop.

– Cop's a cop, he sneered. Then he remembered her dad, and smiled and touched her arm.

Byron told her that Stuart was really happy about, you know. Them. The two of them. Byron said it was a really good thing. He said they were two of his most favourite people, and he was made up to see them together. He said Stuart deserved some happiness. She laughed and asked him what he meant.

– Oh you know.

– More than me?

– No. Just.

– What?

– Oh nothing.

Stuart's parents were still together, but his father was always away and his mother worked in the City and Stuart had the house to himself most of the time and she would go there and they would end up kissing – of course – and they would do various things, but they still hadn't had actual sex. She wondered whether he was really only interested in sex. And was being really clever. And by not ever pressing her into stuff, he made her want stuff that she might not want if he suggested it out loud. Maybe he was devious like that and everything – all his niceness and his calm and the way he looked out for her – was a disguise for the fact that he was just a horny boy like other horny boys and that he was following some sort of Plan and every night he called his friends to bring them up to date about the progress of the Plan.

And even though he never blatantly pushed her into doing anything, he had a way of making her do stuff anyway, by getting the two of them arranged in such-and-such a way and leaving the opportunity open for her to do it if she wanted to, but to not do it if she didn't want to. Which was how she ended up giving her first ever blow job for example. In her life. Which was something that even a couple of months ago she thought she would never do. But now she'd done it. And she had liked it. And it had been completely different to what she had expected, and it had not been gross or embarrassing or weird-tasting or any of the things she had thought it was going to be, and she was doing it even before she'd decided to do it, she was just suddenly doing it, because of the devious way Stuart had arranged their bodies on his bed, with both of them still mostly dressed and the CD by Micachu playing that he'd got for her and that she really liked. Stuart had to stop her almost as soon as she started. He gasped and wriggled and pushed her head away from him and came all over his T-shirt like he'd been shot, and she couldn't help laughing, and then worried almost immediately that he would think she was some sort of *expert*. But all he could say was *wow*, and he laughed too, and they both giggled for a while and he kissed her, and then he took off his T-shirt and mopped up and they hugged and kissed under the covers and laughed at each other and chatted for ages.

He said that no one had ever done that before.

He said that Byron had offered, but that was all.

He said that he and Byron had kissed once, and he had liked it, but he had stopped because he didn't want to do anything else and Byron did, and Byron had sulked for a while, but they were OK again now.

He said Byron was his best friend. Him and Byron talked about everything.

He said she was a better kisser than Byron.

He said he loved her skin and he loved her breasts and her

neck. He said he wanted to hold her every time he saw her in school. He said he'd wanted to kiss her from the first time he'd met her. He said that he had never done anything because she seemed uninterested in him, in that way.

He said he really wanted to have proper sex with her, but there was no hurry.

He said he wasn't a virgin. But he'd only had sex once before and it had been a real mess, a disaster, and he wouldn't tell her who it was, and she didn't know her anyway, and they had both been drunk and it was all a sort of horrible blur of bad memory.

She told him that she was a virgin. He asked about other boys and she told him about some of them. He stroked her hair and smiled at her and they wrapped their legs around each other under the duvet.

She liked him so much that she couldn't do any work.

Her dad came to the house on a Tuesday. 'To speak to your mum', he said, which made her instantly suspicious. Something was up. Something had happened. They talked in the kitchen, and she couldn't hear a thing. It was good, she supposed, that they weren't shouting at each other. But it was creepy too. There wasn't a sound. She tried to work out what it was. He had seen her with Stuart and didn't approve. He was worried that she wasn't doing as well as she had been, at school. Maybe it wasn't about her. He had lost his job. He couldn't afford to pay maintenance any more. He was leaving

London. He had prostate cancer. She sat on the stairs and thought about Stuart having cancer.

He wouldn't tell her what it was about. He seemed impatient. He wanted to be gone.

– See you Saturday?

– Yeah.

– It's not about us. Ask your mother what it's about. She can tell you if she wants. Up to her.

So she had to nag. Her mother was sitting in the kitchen looking at the wall. She had put out mugs but she hadn't filled them. She didn't want to talk about it. Cath whined at her. *What? What's going on?*

– Someone died.

All Cath's breathless wondering stopped. And then restarted.

– Who? What happened?

– Misha. You don't know her. She used to . . . I was at uni with her.

– What happened?

– I don't want to, Cath.

And her mother started crying.

She didn't know what to do. She gave her a sort of hug. She got her a box of tissues. She made a pot of tea. She sat at the table and listened to the story. She caught herself wondering if it was made up. Invented by her mother and father together to warn her of how badly wrong everything could go. Because it was *that* story. About the pretty, clever girl who everyone knows is going to turn out to be a genius but she starts to drink, and then she meets the wrong people, and she drinks too much, and she starts taking other stuff, and before anyone knows what's happened she's living in a junkie squat somewhere in King's Cross and she's got a string of arrests and all her old friends and her traumatized parents are really just waiting for the police to show up at the door to say she's dead. Then she goes away and disappears. She goes to Spain. Years pass. She comes home and she's OK. She's sober and she's done some courses, and everyone thinks that she's better, she's through it. She's not the same, but at least she's not a mess any more, and even if she is a bit fragile, a bit pathetic, she can hold down a sort of office admin job and she can pay rent and it's OK. But she's never what she was. And she's never what she might have been. And they notice that she's probably still drinking. Secretly. And eventually – after everyone stops thinking about her and she has become just a sad friend who doesn't have much of a life and who they never see unless they have to – she hangs herself in her kitchen.

Her mother choked and spluttered on all her guilt and her grief, and she banged the table and cried so loud that Cath was terrified and called her father, but she couldn't reach him, and left an angry message accusing him of being a *heartless bastard*. And her mother might have overheard, because she hugged Cath then and told her *sorry sorry sorry*, she was just *so sad. So sad.* And she went to bed, and Cath could hear her still, wailing, as if she'd lost everything and had nothing left, not even Cath. And then Cath was crying.

She called Stuart. He wanted to come over but she wouldn't let him. She tried to be cold about her mother. She tried to tell him that she was being stupid, but he didn't fall for it, and soon she was crying, and he told her he was coming over, and she told him not to, *thank you*, but she'd prefer if he didn't, because it was her mother, her mother's privacy, and he said OK.

Her dad called. He didn't say anything about being called a heartless bastard, but he didn't apologize either. *She's bound to be upset*, he said. *She'll be OK.* She accused him of not caring. That it was easy for him, it wasn't his friend who had died. And then he was quiet for a minute and told her that actually it was his friend. That he'd known Misha as long as he'd known her mother. That they'd dated a couple of times. And that he'd seen more of her in the last couple of years than anyone else. Cath apologized, and for no reason that she could understand other than having a dig, her father told her that he loved her.

Then there was someone at the door. It was her mother's friend Heather, and then everything was OK. Heather gave her a hug, and went up to her mother. Then their other friends Sean and Lillian arrived. And then everyone was in her mother's bedroom, and coming and going with cups of tea and she even heard laughter.

She called Stuart again. To say sorry. To tell him that everything was OK now. They talked for an hour, each of them lying on their beds. She wrapped his voice around her and made him promise that he wouldn't let her become a junkie. He laughed. OK, he said. I promise. He thought it was a joke. But she knew they would remember it always, that it was a promise to look after her, and that it was made now and could not be retracted, and that even if they did not stay together there were things between them that would never be between her and anyone else. And that wasn't being stupid or romantic or saying that it was *special* or anything. It was just the truth.

She slept late, was late for school. Her mother stayed in bed. Beth nagged at her. Stuart kept an eye on her. Byron asked her was she OK and gave her a hug. She was fine. She was tired. She couldn't remember most of the things she'd talked to Stuart about. She wondered what he'd said to the others. Whether she came across as needy, weepy, clingy. Those things. She ignored him.

She was still annoyed at her dad.

He closed down when he need to be open. That was what she thought. When there was something wrong he became efficient, busy. He dealt with it. Like a policeman. Like you'd want from a policeman. He would arrive and sort it out. Then he'd leave. And it was sorted. It was fixed. It was a closed case and he was closed and everything was shut off and quiet and finished and he forgot about it.

But when there was nothing wrong he was funny and kind and patient and open.

She thought it through again. She wasn't sure what she was complaining about.

It was too hot. They took the tube down through London, holding hands and allowing themselves to be pressed against each other. She had a sheen of sweat on her forehead. Stuart was wearing a T-shirt and kept on lifting and flapping the front over his stomach.

They hadn't been anywhere together for a while. She'd been spending time with her mother, who was still wobbly. She'd sob in front of the television. She'd sit at the kitchen table just staring into space. Cath didn't know why. Well, she knew why, but she didn't understand why the grief was so intense. There was something she didn't know about, she was sure of it. Something more to the story. This Misha. How was it that she had never been spoken of before, and now she was all over Cath's life, even though she was dead. Nothing, then dead, then everything.

Her father came round a few times. More than he had before. He and her mum would sit in the kitchen chatting quietly. She sometimes sat with them for a while. But it was too weird. They just talked to her, about her, while she was there. So she would go and watch television, or go to her bedroom, and she would hear them murmur together for a long time. Once, after she had gone to bed and fallen asleep, the front door woke her. It was her father leaving. She heard his car start up. It was 4.30 in the morning.

She didn't know what it was.

She tried to ask her father. He would not help. All he said was that they'd been good friends once, her mother and this Misha. That was it. She wondered whether they'd been lovers or something. She couldn't imagine it. She wondered whether the three of them had been mixed up in some sort of love triangle thing.

Her father didn't want to talk about it.

It was cruel. It was unfair. She was the one who had to live with her mother. And for a week now she'd been weird and silent and weepy. The day of the funeral, Cath had come home to find her in bed, still wearing her black dress. She'd had to call Heather again. What was wrong with these people? It was like they forgot she existed. As soon as their own stuff hit them, they forgot about her. She had to fend for herself, knowing nothing.

She'd told her father that she couldn't see him that day. That she was seeing Stuart.

They arrived at Waterloo and walked along the river, strolling, holding hands. He looked so good. Byron had said to her a few days before that Stuart was always good-looking, but now that he was going out with her he was beautiful. He'd said it really nicely, quietly, with a big smile. Then he'd made her promise not to tell Stuart he'd said it, or he'd kill her.

The Tate was quiet. There were still tourists and some big groups of kids, but it was nice, it was OK, it was easier to stand and look at things than it usually was. They went searching for the Rothko room. She had told Stuart about Rothko, a little. How he did not move her. And he had wanted to see. He said he knew a song about Rothko by an American singer that he liked. She rolled her eyes. The only things he knew about were things he'd heard in songs. He laughed at her.

They looked at the paintings. The room was almost empty. Large flat blocks of colour frayed at the edges, set against the dark. It was gloomy in there. Why was it so gloomy? It was cool, at least. Cath sat on a bench and tried again with Rothko. Stuart stood at first. Then he sat beside her for a while. They didn't say anything. She wanted to let him decide for himself. He stood up again and walked around the room. Then he stopped in front of one of them and his head dropped on to his chest. Then she saw him wipe his eyes and look up again. She thought he was bored. He didn't get it either. She stood and went to him and took his hand, meaning to lead him out of the room so they could look at some other stuff or get a coffee. He turned to her. He was crying. Not sobbing. But there were a couple of tears running down the side of his nose, and his eyes were red. She stared at him.

He wanted to stay in the room. He moved around. She watched him. He breathed deeply. He stood still. Really still. He sat on the seats a couple of times and just looked. She wondered if he was taking the piss. She went and sat beside him.

– What do you think?

– They're beautiful. I don't understand how they work. But they're just beautiful.

He wanted to stay there for ages. He looked at the Rothkos, and she looked at him.

In the café afterwards she complained about her parents. She told him that there was something they weren't telling her about this dead woman, Misha. She told him it wasn't fair. That they just weren't thinking about her. He nodded.

– Maybe they can't, he said.

– They could try.

– Maybe you had to be there. Some things you can't share, you know?

He got a second coffee. He wanted to talk about the Rothko room. He seemed a bit embarrassed now, that he'd been so moved by it. He smiled and shook his head.

– They're so great though. I could look at those things all day.

She told him about her dad and the eggs.

– I made my dad scrambled eggs one morning yeah? When I was staying in his place for a weekend. He sleeps late you know. And I made him breakfast when he got up, you know – good little girl. And it was like, scrambled eggs on toast, and some bacon and a tomato. Stuff like that. And a pot of tea. Glass of orange juice. All posh. And he really liked it. And then he was trying to show off that he knew about art – he's always doing this – and he splatters ketchup all over the scrambled eggs and he said, *Rothko eggs*. Pointing at the eggs yeah? *Rothko eggs*. I didn't know what he was on about. *They look like a Rothko painting*, he said, all pleased with himself. And then I realized that he'd gotten Rothko mixed up with Pollock!

She laughed.

Stuart smiled.

– So now he still calls scrambled eggs *Rothko eggs*. I never corrected him. He hasn't realized yet. So he's always asking for *Rothko eggs*. I bet he does it at work and everything. Trying to show off how cultured he is. Down the police station, you know? Pretending he knows his art. *Had some great Rothko eggs this morning*. And no one has a clue what he's on about. It's so funny.

And she laughed, to show how funny it was.

Stuart smiled at her. He looked at her and smiled and said nothing, and he rubbed his eyes.

Later that day she asked him about the scar.

– What happened?

– What?

– There. How did you get it?

– Shark bite.

– Really though.

He said nothing for a minute. Then he lay on his back and looked at the ceiling.

– A few years ago. I was swimming in a river. Sort of a river thing, near where we were staying on holiday in France. Me and a friend went swimming. He was a local guy. And we got snagged on some stuff under the water. There was some old farm machinery or something dumped in there. And we were kind of diving down and exploring it. It wasn't very deep but we were trying to . . . I don't know . . . pretending it was a shipwreck or something. He pushed a bit of it I think. Or pulled it. Or maybe he didn't. But it shifted. We got . . .

He stopped.

– What?

– Some part of it caught my leg when I was freeing myself. Some sharp edge. And cut it.

– Shit. Did it hurt?

– Yeah. Well. Yeah, after a bit. I didn't notice at first.

– 'Cos you have arteries and stuff in there. You could bleed to death.

– Yeah.

He said nothing. She looked at him.

He was quiet. He had drifted off somewhere. She traced shapes and words and pictures on his chest with her fingers. The sun lit the curtains and the music made her drowsy. She was lulled by his heartbeat into feeling nothing more than a vague wonder that nothing in her life had really started yet.

She went home. She thought about their day. Something had gone wrong but she didn't know what.

Marching Songs

I am ill. I have been ill for some time. Years now. It has become years.

I believe, though I cannot prove, that my illness is due directly to the perverted Catholicism and megalomania of Mr Tony Blair, former Prime Minister, whom I met once, whose hand I physically shook (at which point he assaulted me), and who, if you should mention my name to him, will tell you that he met me, or that he did not meet me, or that he cannot recall. Because he has all the answers.

My illness is debilitating. It disbars me from work. It prevents any social interaction. It has been, my illness, both mis-recognized and dismissed. Misdiagnosed. And dismissed. As malingering; as a problem of my own creation, of my own invention, as if it was my child or my garden or a song I was singing, or something I have idly, on a quiet afternoon say, made up, invented, as a story to tell mental health profes-sionals because I have nothing better to do. It generates anger, pity, bloody-minded stinking compassion, notes between doctors, phone calls and files, avoidance, the disappearance of friends, and all that sort of Englishness. I sit in my chair.

Compassion is a weapon wielded against me. Amongst others.

I'm not blaming you, specifically. I don't blame people, specifically.

However, Islington council, my landlords, my sister (against her entire knowledge), and the NHS are all trying to kill me. Trying to enable circumstances (to arise) in which my death becomes inevitable. They are involved in an unconscious, unarticulated conspiracy to kill me in other words. It's not a plot. It's nothing so straightforward as a plot. No one can be blamed in any individual way. It is an inevitable, bureaucratic conspiracy, so devolved and deniable as to be invisible; so peculiarly set out in rules and procedures and protocols and directives and guidelines as to allow plausible public denial of responsibility on the part of any of the participants at any stage of the process.

Initiated by Mr Blair. Of which I have no proof. A small wart. On my thumb. It sings to me in the mornings in warm weather. My doctor shrugs at it, and no ointment works.

No blame. You understand me. When they write the report, my report, the report into my case, they will find some systemic failures, some culture of this or that, some procedures for tightening, some lessons to be learned. No heads will roll. Dead children. You understand me.

*

I like where I live. I live on my own.

It's not necessary to be paranoid or to harbour any delusions in order to feel that I have been abandoned by the mental health services. Because I have. They want me to fail, mentally. I have innumerable documents if that sort of thing interests you. Tracing a clear trajectory of discouragement, in which a subtle strategy is discernible. No single thing. Cumulative. Terribly slow, terribly patient. The gentle whisper of the letters and the reports and the assessments. *Die*, they say. You may as well.

My GP, one example, has prescribed to me, for the pain, enough Tramadol to kill me several times over. Go on. Another example, the mental health doctor who first assessed me in Archway had an office on what appeared to be the 12th floor, with a large window, and she sat me within easy reach of the window and also left me alone for several minutes in the room with the window on the 12th floor, which had a view of all of the east or south or west of London from Archway. All that sky, like the city is upside down. So that if you stepped out there you would rise. Several minutes. Perhaps seven or eight. Go on.

I do not have any trouble with my neighbours and I have never had any complications with either the police or the security services, nor have I ever stood for elected office or campaigned for any political party nor have I ever agitated or demonstrated against the authorities in any way, not even on a march – and I never even went on the anti-war march – so there can be no reason for what is happening to me that is public or which may have been expected to arise as a result of my previous actions. I can only assume that the council and my landlords and the NHS have an occult agenda to which they secretly adhere, created for them by the Tony Blair government, to encourage into complete despair any person who does not hold a stake in the national project involving bank accounts for babies, education for profit, and pretending to fight wars – when in fact all that is happening in Afghanistan, and all that happened in Iraq, is that British soldiers are invested in American projects so that the Tony Blair Agenda can feel that it is a stakeholder in the future, which it cannot imagine as being anything other than American, and this is our national embarrassment.

I am not a stakeholder. I hold no stake. I pay my taxes. My taxes buy weapons and arm soldiers. My taxes send the soldiers to Afghanistan and formerly Iraq to be terrified and traumatized, and to inflict terror and trauma upon others, including the killing and maiming of others, and I do not support Our Boys, it is a volunteer army and I believe that every one of those volunteers is misguided and that their innate, childish, boyish attraction to aggression and adventure and camaraderie is being perverted by malign and morally vacant politicians who are not even clever enough to be operating to anyone's advantage, not even their own, who are merely drunk on narrative and who see themselves as part of something bigger, such as the delusion of History, and who are impressive only in the scope and depth and profundity of their stupidity.

He's quite charming, actually, Mr Blair, when you meet him. You can see how he manages to draw people to him. He looks you in the eye. He listens. His smile is warm and he is the right height – neither too tall nor too short. The average height of successful politicians is five feet eleven.

My landlords make noise at a very early hour meaning that I cannot sleep. They also send in the middle of the night an overweight middle-aged or elderly man who tries the steel doors. He rattles them. The landlords, let me explain, have their offices below my flat. I never speak to the head man. He never speaks to me. But I see him, dapper and small, coming and going, and I see how they defer to him and I notice, I have noticed, how he watches me sometimes with half a smile. He has an odd name – Mishazzo. An unlikely name. As if he is a landlord by mistake. His people are very polite, even friendly. But they are, as soon as I am inside my flat, extremely devious in their methods, always doing things that are small enough in themselves but which taken together amount to a campaign of psychological torture, including slamming doors. I think they have fed rats into the cavities. Certainly the cat that used to patrol the yard has disappeared. There are noises in the walls, in the roof, the ceiling. My ceiling is the roof. I hear scratches. Scurries. I hear clicks. I once found a cockroach in my bathroom. I ran downstairs and into the landlord's office but they were not of any use at all to me . . . in me . . . in my horror. Mr Mishazzo was there. His people glanced at him and he smiled. As if he is a landlord because he finds it amusing. Mr Price came by later with a trap. I wanted nothing to do with a trap. I have devices now. Electronic discouragers. Since I have installed them there have been no further creatures inside apart from mosquitoes, bluebottles, wasps, flies, tiny centipedes, moths, a spider.

I have some sort of infection in my forehead.

Let me level with you. Level best and utmost. Let me be as honest as I can be. I know that something has gone wrong. I know that the fault is visible. You can discern it in everything I say to you. In most of what I say to you. In how I say it. I know this. I am cracked like ice. I know this. But listen. Listen to me. This is important. Beneath the fault there is solid ground. Beneath the ice. Under all the cracks. Under all the cracks there is something that is not broken.

I am on the Internet.

You can watch the suicide bombers on there.

I go down to the square a couple of times a week.

Giggling now.

On the Internet, you can watch people dying, all over the place. This is new, isn't it? This is a new thing in the world. On a slow day, when nothing happens, I wait for the news, hoping that there will be something happening there. And sometimes there is. And I like the idea of something happening. I like the idea of it. People don't take anything seriously unless something is happening. My illness makes more sense when something is happening. Against the background of light entertainment and the weather it looks inappropriate. It sticks out. Against the background of body parts and the constant slaughter it looks wise and cautious and who could blame me? I imagine that if there were lots of things happening to me all the time I would like the idea of nothing happening. Sometimes the news is nothing. So much happens and they tell us nothing. I look out of the window.

When I met Tony Blair we talked briefly about motor racing. About Formula One. I don't know why. There had been a Grand Prix that day. It came up somehow. Someone else mentioned it. I said oh. I said I used to watch Formula One as a boy. Not any more? the Prime Minister asked me.

No.

Not any more. Nothing happens now. In Formula One.

Through my window I can't see very much of what I suppose is the world. Some offices. A roof. A sky crossed by planes. I often hear helicopters but I don't see them. There is always something happening. If I press my cheek against the glass and twist my shoulder to the left I can see the elderly or overweight man rattling the steel door. No helicopters. Just the street and the orange lights, wet sometimes. The wet orange street. Shining in the dark and the rattling door.

When nothing is happening we want something to

happen, and when something is happening we want it to stop.

There is always something happening on the Internet.

I sit at my kitchen table. I make a cup of tea.

The Zapruder film. Hillsborough. Bloody Sunday. The shooting of Oswald. The audio of Bobby Kennedy's murder. The calls from the towers. The planes going in. The jumpers. The suicide of Pennsylvania State Treasurer Budd Dwyer on live television. He stuck a gun in his mouth and blew the back of his head off. The camera zooms in on his dead face, the blood pouring out of him like the water out of my overfilled kettle. I don't know what to do about it.

The Madrid bombs. Running up those stairs. The Enschede explosion. Laughter then fear then the world just goes dark and sideways.

Tamil suicide bombers flinging parts of their bodies into the crowd like pop stars.

Iraqi IEDs. Hostage murders. Car bombs by the Green Zone.

Hundreds of dead people. Around craters in Baghdad, Tikrit and Ramadi. British armaments. American armaments. You can see the markings and the peeled-back steel.

There are photographs of aftermaths. Blood and stumps and crushed torsos. All the devil's little mandibles. Misery hats. Pockets of tissue. Cups of tea. There are interviews with people in shock. They cannot begin to believe what they have seen until they tell someone else what they have seen. They shout at the camera, they use their hands, they say things over and over. They're actually talking to themselves, and we are watching.

I am talking to myself and you are watching.

In my kitchen I can look at the wall if I want to.

When he shook hands I felt a sort of scratch. A nick. A prick. Something or other. I didn't react. I didn't look at my hand. I was meeting the Prime Minister. But it hurt. Something had. He had. I don't know.

Some device.

There are endless car crashes on the Internet. There are head-on collisions, turnovers, side swipes, flying pedestrians. All sorts, really. But it is usually unclear whether there have been fatalities.

I stare at the little wart on my thumb. It's white. Tiny and a perfect circle.

When I go down to the square I take a coffee with me, in my hand. I get it from the coffee shop around the corner. I glance at the machine gun policemen. I walk through the square, as if I have business on the other side. They keep an eye on me. I nod sometimes at a policeman. A policeman sometimes nods back. I haven't spotted the cameras. I expect they will knock on my door sometime. That they will come and have a chat.

I'll examine their cards. Their IDs. I'll look at their faces and their photos. They won't mind me writing down the numbers. I'll do it at the kitchen table, so that they follow me into the flat. Let them have a good look around. They'll stand over me. Looking. Two of them. They'll smell of the street and of cars and of camaraderie in the locker room and the gym and of encounters with trouble.

— You think I don't live well?

— What? No. We're here about Connaught Square.

— About what?

— Connaught Square.

— What the hell is a connocked square?

I'll have them baffled in minutes. I'll speak slightly louder than is necessary. I'll walk them backwards through a prayer. Policemen are standard procedures. There is nothing to them that cannot be confused.

— You took your time getting here.

— What?

— I called you hours ago.

— We're not responding to a call.

— So you know about the windows?

— What about the windows?

— They are haunted.

— Haunted?

— They contain reflections at night other than my own.

— Ghosts?

— What are you going to do about it?

And so on.

I go and sit in the park. There is a view over the City, and to the left, Canary Wharf. The park is full of people looking in the same direction.

Part of managing my illness is to keep. Is to try to keep. Is to try to manage to keep a certain amount of regularity in my operations, my whereabouts. A structure. When the pains allow. When the singing isn't outrageous. I used to work in radio. Everything had a schedule. I try to get up every morning and I do. I get up at eight o'clock and I listen for a little while to the *Today* programme. I never worked on that. I try to have a shower. Sometimes I am in too much pain to shower. Sometimes I just get dressed and think about having a bath later. I never have a bath.

I go to Sparrow's for my breakfast. I have Breakfast #5, except I have black pudding instead of beans, and I have tea and toast. I try to take my time. It costs four pounds. I can't afford to do this every day, so sometimes I stay in bed. The waitress calls the toast bread when she brings it. Not every morning, but most. There is a man there, sometimes, two times in four maybe. A small man in a thoughtless suit, short haired, crooked somehow. I look at him trying to work out what it is. I think maybe he's had a harelip corrected. Maybe it's just a broken nose. Some facial thing from childhood like a ghost. He has scrambled eggs. Every time I see him he has scrambled eggs in front of him. A hill of yellow rubble, as if he's been sick. He has a notebook that he writes in sometimes. Maybe he's a writer or a journalist. I'm trying to work out if he's some sort of writer or journalist. Sometimes he reads a newspaper, a tabloid usually, but he doesn't read the same newspaper every time, which is more evidence that he might be a journalist, I think. He is half ugly half handsome. He looks at his watch. Sometimes he talks on his phone, turning the pages of the newspaper, or writing lazily in his notebook, making humming noises, *yes, go on, yes, OK.* He's the only regular I notice. I don't think he notices me. Who would look at me?

I look at him. Sometimes I think he's crying, which makes me laugh. Sometimes I think that night is day and I look out of the window and everything is wrong until I realize it's night and this is what the night is like.

The man who rattles the steel door and shutters. That's always in the middle of the night. I lift the corner of my curtain and peek at him. He is big. He wears a grey jacket. In the dark it's grey. He just rattles the door, the shutters. He does it and he stands there for a moment staring at the steel. And then he goes away. I don't know what it's about. Perhaps he has a grievance.

When I go outside into the street where I live I am surrounded by people shouting and jostling and buying vegetables. That's OK. Where did they get their lives? Who told them that this was the way to be? How did they learn? They are pushed up against one another with no space for anything. They have become unhealthy and short minded. Things move so quickly that they don't know what to do with anything, other than shout at it or push it or try to buy it.

In the past I drew down from the local people all the things I needed. All the things I needed were things I needed to draw down, to pull down into me, like fruit on a branch. Along my street I met with grocers and barbers and phone-fixing men. I ambled slowly into furniture shops and asked them about the price of hatstands and bunk beds. I paused in butcher's doorways and stared at meat counters, at the cuts of flesh and the granulated blood. I licked my lips in the windows. I walked the street I live on. What is this vegetable? What is this fruit? What is the name you call this? How do I cook it? I took time in cafés where they fed me. I watched other people. I listened in on other people. I read sometimes. I didn't read.

I have lost my place now. I do none of that.

If he is a journalist I might tell him about Blair and the device. A pin. A poisoned pin. Or a miniature syringe. Some sort of nano-technology. His hand was dry. His smile was the one you've seen on the television. The same one. Except we were in a room, and there were no cameras. Odd.

All the deaths in Formula One are on the Internet. Most of them are. Most of them after about 1967. Gilles Villeneuve and Ronnie Peterson and Ayrton Senna. Villeneuve thrown from his car. The medics crouched over his broken body caught against the fence. Peterson pulled burning from a multiple pile up at Monza. They didn't think he was badly hurt. He died hours later when his bone marrow melted into his bloodstream. Senna. Going straight ahead into concrete. They still don't know why. It takes a slow two minutes for the medics at Imola to get to him. On the American commentary Derek Daly worries about the delay. *Where are they?* he asks. Tom Pryce in 1973 – he hits a marshal who is running across the track, the marshal's body spinning in the air like wet bread, his fire extinguisher hitting Pryce's helmet, shattering it, killing Pryce instantly, though his car continues in a straight line. Jochen Rindt, 1970, Monza. It doesn't look that bad. Lorenzo Bandini's Ferrari exploding by the yachts in Monaco. It looks that bad.

Riccardo Paletti on the starting line at Monza in 1982. He slams into the back of Didier Pironi's Ferrari which has stalled in pole position. The other drivers have managed to avoid it. But Paletti doesn't see it. They say that he's dead by the time the marshals and the medics and Pironi get to his car, but still. You can watch the film. You can watch them trying to get Paletti out. You can see the moment when the first flames appear. If you listen to the version with Jackie Stewart's commentary you can hear the panic in his voice when the flames suddenly take hold, bursting over the whole car, sending everyone scurrying, and you can watch then as a collection of flailing useless men try to make the extinguishers work and Ricardo Paletti burns.

Roger Williamson at Zandvoort in 1973. He flips his March on the long corner and he's trapped inside it. A fire starts. His friend David Purley sees what's happened, stops his car, runs across the track and tries to help. He tries to lift the car. He gestures to the marshals to help him. They aren't wearing fire-proof clothing. They hang back. He gestures at other cars. They think it's Purley's car that's overturned. And they can see Purley, so everything must be OK, and they're racing, so they don't stop. Purley can hear Roger Williamson. He can hear him shouting. Then screaming. The extinguisher won't work. There's only one. He tries to get it to work. He tries to lift the car. He can't lift the car. The marshals are standing there looking at him. The smoke is billowing out. The race goes on. He walks away. He runs back. His arms. His shoulders. He can hear Williamson. Then he can't.

You can watch it all. Over and over.

I watch it all, over and over.

Several items arising. The local health and mental health unit of the Borough of Islington have now discontinued my therapy a total of twice on two separate occasions, ruling that I was in both of these times incapable of benefiting, using this deception to cover over like a dog their ineptitude and possible encouragement of my self destruction, ignoring on three separate occasions my stated intention to kill someone, preferably Mr Blair or someone else like that, deciding that these were not serious threats and were instead manifestations of my own particular 'illness', as if the world was separate from the things in it, the events separate from the people, the people separate from the things they do, as if the done things do not come out of thought things, as if there were no traces anywhere, as if we had never noticed dogs and the way they proceed. What a remarkable ambush of shit. What a cloud of frayed cities. What a dust of blood. What a wound. What a pulse of broken teeth. I will fucking kill you. I WILL FUCKING KILL. YOU FUCK.

I am ugly. Ugliness has taken me over. It's OK. The infection in my forehead has spread along the slight left centre of my nose and out into my left cheek. My right cheek. The slight right centre of my nose and my right cheek. I have red cleft marks along my thighs and under my right arm. One eye has failed. It rarely opens now. There is a stench inside my mouth. There are ruins in my corners. I cannot wash and carry on.

There is the problem of money.

When I left my job – left, left, I had a good job but I left – they gave me a certain amount, which I stored in a savings account, an ISA account, where you are allowed to put only a certain amount of money in different ways and you do not have to pay tax on what you earn there. That is my under-standing. And the rest of it I put in another account which is an ordinary savings account and it earns interest in there and I suppose that somehow I pay tax on that though perhaps I don't pay taxes any longer. I'm not sure. There's the principle of it though. Then there was the house I had. I sold. I sold the house I had. That's OK. All that money I put mostly in another savings account and another current account and all this money is all nearly gone now I'm sure of it, though my sister looks after my finances for the moment for the most part, and she hasn't said anything, yet, except to get a job. But she says that gently now. These days. I am disfigured.

I will go and stand by the café. And watch them. They come and go. The policemen. By the square. He spent millions on the house. It's in the public record. You can look it up. It's where he lives. With his armed guard and his devices and all his perpetual shame, poor man. Sometimes I feel sorry for him.

Money is a problem. I find that I cannot spend it when I go out. I go out and I go to the shops, for example, and I try to buy food. I walk around the shop, the supermarket, with a basket on my arm, and I put things in it. Milk for example, bread, eggs, some pasta, some mushrooms and carrots, some orange juice, a fillet of fish or a pork chop. I fill the basket. I put in extra things that might be nice like some buns or a cake or a packet of biscuits. Extra things that might be nice. But when I get to the checkout I cannot. I cannot. In the air. My pains all sing their song. I cannot take the money out of my pocket. I cannot take the items one by one from the basket and have them sent under the bleeper. It cannot happen. This is so stupid. This is mad. There is something wrong with it. Something horrible. I don't know what it is. I stand in the queue for a moment, maybe longer, and I try to stay, but I put the basket down and I leave – I go to the door and through it and the security guard looks at me and shakes his head.

Cash. I have a problem with cash.

I think.

In Sparrow's though, for my breakfast, I can do that. Because it is four pounds. £4. It is always £4. So I have that ready. Or, I know the change I will get. A one-pound coin. Or a five-pound note and a one-pound coin. The crooked man in the suit does the same. He knows the price of scrambled eggs. It's the way to do it. It really is.

And I can get a coffee when I go down to the square. I can do that. It is £1.85 in the place I get it. I give them £2. They give me 15p change. I drop that in the glass they leave on the counter for tips.

My bills are paid automatically. I'm on the Internet. And that will do. I have lost weight. My fingers sing to me. My sister comes on Saturdays and she brings what I more or less need.

Once I had an urge for cornflakes, and I stole them from the corner shop. I had no milk. I went back and bought milk. I don't know how I did it. I think I forgot that I was unable to use cash. I think I forgot – so perplexed was I by the theft – that I was mad. I wanted to pay him for the cornflakes too but he didn't know what I was on about, and he shooed me out of it like more than two schoolchildren.

I watch them in the café. By the square. Down by the square. The same place I get the £1.85 coffee. There are several of them. They know I'm there. I'm sure. They have that training. Things attached to their belts. They don't mind me then. They don't mind me so much I don't think. Maybe they don't see me. Maybe it's another division that sees me.

David Purley was born in Bognor Regis of all places. I have never been there.

Soldiers sing as they march. They sing as they march.

In his car as he burned to death Roger Williams sang. David Purley never mentioned it. He thought he was hearing things. He thought, when he remembered it, that he was making it up, that such a thing was ridiculous, that it was impossible, that it was impossible and wrong to remember it, so he never mentioned it. He never said a word. Roger had sung. Sang. Roger sang.

I am going to get better.

He sang a melody that Purley had never heard before. I don't know what it was. Something lovely. Purley sang it himself when he crashed his aerobatic biplane into the sea in 1985. Off Bognor Regis of all places, in sight of home. He remembered the melody that Roger had sung. Sang. And he sang it too. It is a death song, I suppose. Death needs its orders, its boots, its motivations. Death needs its rations.

Poor death.

My sister brings most of the food I need. It lasts the week. I am embarrassed more than anything about my sister. About myself in relation to my sister.

I am tired of talking.

The pains in my stomach are now sometimes unbearable. I listen to them sing. The pains, I mean. They sing. They keep themselves chipper with songs. Because it is hard to be a pain in me. It is hard work. It takes all day to use up a minute of my time. It takes a great effort of all those little pains, working together, to make the song, the chorus, that sounds in my head like a world. These days they have learned their song and they seem happy in their work and they can on a good day lay me low and kill me. They kill me and I die. And I am resurrected.

What did I say to him? To Mr Blair? What statement did I make, what question did I ask to prompt his attack on me? Or was it something in my face or my bearing or in my eyes. Something in my eyes? Was it a story I told, of something in my life? Was it a joke I made? What did I do to Mr Blair? What offence or danger did I present? What was it about me that led to his decision? Perhaps nothing. Perhaps it was an accident of timing. He felt the need to destroy something. Anything. Given his power. It would be a sin, perhaps he thought, not to use it.

Maybe he felt I would be better off.

He thinks a lot, I imagine, about sin. Uselessly.

Death will come to him as a terrible shock, I shouldn't wonder.

Maybe he detected my unhappiness in my work. My unhappiness at home. Maybe he felt that I would be better off with all that misery behind me. Maybe he felt that my life needed shaking up. That I could do with a shock, upending and run through. The pains started the very next day, when I woke. I could not move. I could not move for days. All my limbs, my joints, my knuckles and my hairs, all my ducts and patches. They were all tuning up.

The man in Sparrow's looked at me blankly.

– What?

– Are you a journalist or a writer?

He had a settled face. A man in control of his expressions. I couldn't read anything in there. He'd finished his eggs, his toast. His plate was pushed aside. He had a second mug of tea on the go. Did he do that every morning? I didn't know. He was reading about global warming in the newspaper. There was a picture of a glacier and sidebars with explanations. His phone sat on his notebook. There'd been no calls this morning, and no writing either. His voice was level. I couldn't get the accent. Flat south-east. London, out of Essex or Kent. I don't know. His face wasn't as crooked up close. Odd that. I find it difficult to talk to people.

– I'm neither.

– I thought you might be. A writer. A journalist. With the notebook. You know.

He nodded, slowly.

– No.

– OK.

I didn't know where that left me. If he said he wasn't then he wasn't. I couldn't start an argument about it.

– I've seen you in here, you know. With the notebook. Writing. The odd time. I just thought. We're often in at the same time.

He nodded again. Maybe he was tired. He looked tired and sad and red-eyed. He didn't seem to mind, but he wasn't going to talk to me. He wasn't going to ask me to sit down. He wasn't going to ask me to sit down and tell him about Mr Blair and the device so that he could tell my story.

I thought I would tell him my name. I'd say my name, my surname, and I'd hold out my hand for him to shake. And I'd smile, and he'd pause and smile back and take my hand and ask me to sit down. So, *we eat breakfast here,* he'd say. Or. *You must be local, too.* Or something like that. A small talk interregnum. Then down to it. I'd duck into it. I'd use dialogue. I'd speak in dialogue. In lines. *You want to hear a story?* I'd say. He'd shrug. *Politics,* I'd say. *Politicians. Not quite what they seem, sometimes.* I'd pause. *Go on,* he'd say. *You remember Blair?* Interested. *Of course I remember Blair. What about him?*

And so on.

I didn't know what to say.

– Well. Nice to talk to you.

He nodded again.

– Bye now.

– Bye.

He sipped his tea and looked at me. I walked to the door and out on to the street. I don't know. I don't know what to do with the rest of my life.

Mr Blair is not the owner of his own evil. He is the host if you like – if you want to use the sort of terminology that he has adapted into his own life and heart, the vocabulary of the groping church – he is the possessed corpse of a former human, animated entirely by the spittle-flecked priests of Rome and by miserable justifications, by ointments of the sagging flesh, the night-time coldness of the awful touch. His skin is a manila envelope. It contains an argument, not a heart. But he has made choices and the choices are owned by him, and he owns those choices and he is the chooser of death. He is the chooser of death. He has chosen death and he has chosen to visit it on others when no such choice was necessary. He is the progenitor of the crushed skulls of baby girls. He is the father of the dead bodies of children and the raped mothers and the bludgeoned fathers. He has embraced the murder of his lord, and he has used the people to enact his fantasy and his perversions. He has masturbated over the Euphrates. He has rubbed History against his cold chest like a feeler in the crowd. Like a breather, interferer. Slack muscle of pornography, piece of shit.

I only know what I believe.

I go down sometimes to the square, and I wander with a coffee and I watch and I go around again. Nothing happens. I have to be careful. Even still, I'm sure I'm noticed.

I saw him once. Early in the day as I came from Marble Arch. He was no more than a blur between his house and his car; a man in a suit, moving as if it was raining, crouching out, ducking in. I stopped in my tracks. Words rose in my throat. I had no idea. I didn't know what to do. It was such a beautiful morning.

He glanced in my direction and I saw his face. He did not look at me but I saw his face. He looked terribly familiar. Of course. But no. Not as himself. He wears a state of shock. He carries panic in his eyes. He bristles with tension and fear, as if he knows what he does not want to know – that any moment now, it will be too late.

I went home and slept.

There are too many photographs of David Purley attending to the dying of his friend Roger Williamson. There is too much film. His human body makes too much of itself, changing direction, pausing, giving up, resuming, going back, tensing in fear, resuming, slumping in despair, ragged in despair, resuming, going back, screaming, his voice, you can see his voice in the pictures, screaming, *somebody fucking help me, somebody fucking help.*

There are two sorts of pale skinny Englishmen in my nightmares. One is burned at the edges, frayed by fear, his blistered hands and scorched face taut with the effort of trying to save a life. David Purley. And the other, a coward and a traitor, who set his face against bravery, who embraced the dying man and swallowed his song. Tony Blair.

Tony Blair.

I wake to the rattling and the marching songs.

The Association of
Christ Sejunct

The poisoned evening spun a little. The sky was pink and the buildings black and the lights looked wet in the warmth, and people trickled out of the tube station like beads of sweat. He didn't want to breathe. On his tongue he tasted distant cooking or the drains.

He had stopped shouting.

He looked at the sky. It was not far. He stamped his right foot to get his boot back on and thought of the soldiers by the cross and the grey and purple clouds closing over them and what they must have thought about. Very simple things. Supper. Money. Fucking.

The sky.

A police car turned the corner, silent but the lights flashing. He watched it creep towards him, its tyres hissing on the soft tarmac. He stood on the kerb and the car passed him. He stamped his foot. It stopped. A man got out looking bored but well equipped. He could smell plastic, and fresh sweat seeping through old deodorant. He stamped again. The man affixed a complicated belt to his waist. Tightened it. Fastened it.

– Hello, sir.

He said nothing. Looked at him. White man with red lips, cold skin. He smelled so clean. His arms met his body in a tuft of scented turf and he was straight from the television. Or the gym or the back of a magazine.

– We had a call about some shouting?

He stamped his boot.

The shopkeeper appeared. The taste of butter. The small ankles of his wife's bullshit figurines. There was chatter by his left ear. Back there somewhere. His wife would be sitting in the armchair. She would be clutching the first of her Coca-Colas and marking out the television in the *Standard*. Back there somewhere. He moaned. He raised his mouth to the sky and wanted to wail and nothing came but moaning.

– Right. Sir. Can you tell me your name please?

Some boys had gathered opposite.

– What is it, bruv? What's he done, man?

The driver emerged and gestured and walked around the car. Circumauto. Another belt. Their shirts were white but they wore . . . things over them. Chest pieces. Armour. The sky's pink darkened. The sky. He must forget about the sky for the moment.

Vests. Stab vests. He flexed his right thigh.

– My wife, he said.

– What's your name please, sir?

He didn't want to give his name.

– My wife is at home.

– Good for her.

He looked straight up. He was afraid that he wouldn't do it. If he didn't do it, no one would know that he'd planned to do it.

– Been having a bit of a shout have we?

He could hear the shopkeeper at his shoulder, giving an account. This and this. The boys across the road wheeled in tiny circles on a tiny bike, bounced a football, dislocated their hips, pushed laughter between themselves like a pool game – angles, ricochets, trick shots. Hats. Were they not too hot? The shopkeeper spoke low but he could hear the accusations and the falsehoods and the traps. Menace. Shouting. A disturbance. Scaring customers. Creating a scene.

He wouldn't argue.

His wife was diabetic.

He would not shift. His toes on the edge of the kerb. His heels on the path. His hands by his side. His head tilted upwards.

– Can you move over here a little, please?

– My wife is diabetic.

– All right. What's your name?

– I don't want to tell you.

– You know why I've stopped you?

– You haven't stopped me.

They had notebooks. They wore tags and emblems. Little silver pokes of office, he supposed. Their fabric was soft black, their shirts crisp; there were various things on their belts. He was straining his eyes. Peeking. He returned to the lowering sun and thought of naked boys by the stable, running knives through each other's hair. He could smell bare skin.

– Are you arresting me?

– I'm trying to talk to you.

– I'm armed.

There was a gap.

– With what?

– Leave me be.

Oh Jesus! He was a small framed creature now, with his hair longer than the other boys, longer than his mother liked, and he ran in the evenings by the river with the other boys, with their low calls and whistles, a little language of the river at sunset that they had invented for themselves, and Jesus ran faster than them all, and they stripped and spent time in the water, and still stripped they crept up on the girls in the new dark, the girls around the . . . campfire? He didn't know. He saw the girls around a little fire. Working on clothing. They were working on clothing somehow. Mending clothes and making clothes. Robes and gowns and the things people wore then. And he saw the boys in the dark, and the girls knowing the game and thinking it, for the most part, boyish and disgusting and stupid. But sometimes they peered into the gloom at the naked shapes, and held their breath at the moans and the laughs and the gulped air. Jesus liked to listen with his eyes closed. He could hear the breath of everyone, and knew what it meant. He knew how their minds were directed, their disguised intentions, their thoughts. One boy always stood close to him, always sought him out. One girl was sick, her head reeled in the flickering light and she wanted to be dead. Another girl battled with herself and prayed, her heart split open, flooded with fear and despair, thinking that this was her test. This was not her test. Most of the girls breathed bored or excited breaths, their words matching their thoughts, for the most part. Most of the boys breathed excitement, though there was some doubt too, and fear, and one boy hated himself and his friends and his hate wrestled with his lust, and both of them were strange to him, and he spat on his hand as if spitting on an enemy.

Jesus was surrounded by the breath of others.

The policemen had taken a step back, and the shopkeeper had disappeared.

– I'm going to ask you to put your hands behind your back, OK?

– You arresting me?

– Yes, I'm arresting you.

– No.

He spun to his left with his arm extended and he thought he did it fast but he met only empty air and then something had a hold of his wrist. He raised his arm, raised it, raised it, and the policeman let go and he turned and he ran. He ran. His legs were strong. His shirt flapped and his jeans caught on his thighs and his boots were imperfect. But he ran. He could run. He could run faster than any policeman. He smiled. He was going towards the tube. At least one of them was after him. Perhaps both of them. No, only one of them. The other would be on the radio. He slammed into a woman at the entrance and she went flying and he turned a sharp left and he could hear the boys shouting and laughing *Yeah man, run bruv, run blud run! Fuck the feds man, fuck em!* and he came out of the second entrance and ran through the bus park to the main road and right, under the bridges, and he was just warming up now. He glanced back. Still there.

People looked small and still when he ran.

His wife had started with cartoon characters. Not so many. That was fine. Then she had gone on to historical personages. Little things. Made of something or other. Porcelain. A couple of inches high. Six inches high. On pedestals or bases made to look like scenes. Tree stumps. Motor cars. Robin Hood. Dick Whittington. Peter Rabbit. Florence Nightingale. Princess Diana. The first time they had sex they were fifteen years old and it was summer like this. She had Barack Obama now.

He could taste the trains.

He took the road at a long angle and the cars parted for him.

He went left again, into the park. Up the little hill. Left again. He cut the grassy corners. Jesus would run for hours. He would run what we would call marathons, all around his village. Longer than that. Bursts of speed when he wanted. Past the skateboard place where a couple of shirtless white boys stopped in the gloom and stared at him, but they had short hair; and past the tennis courts where some people turned and looked. He glanced back again. The policeman was flagging.

He needed someone to talk to.

He went left again. He was making a circle. He went across the narrow bridge over the railway tracks. He screamed a woman with a pram out of his way. When he got to the other side he stopped. He ducked to the right and he drew the knife. Then he stepped out and faced back across the bridge. The policeman. No one else. The policeman, red-faced, distorted. He started to run. Towards him. Fast. His knife flashing in the dusk, catching yellow from the track lights. The policeman slowed, hesitated, stopped, turned, shouted something, ran back the way he had come.

– Don't cross this fucking bridge. Hear me? Set foot on this fucking bridge I fucking kill you.

He stopped. He kicked the sides. He kicked the fucking sides. He walked backwards. He could hear the click and hiss of the radio. He could taste his own breathlessness rise in his throat. Say it. He swallowed.

– This bridge is mine. Mine, you hear me? Step on and I shoot.

He went back to the other side. He could see the policeman's head peering at him. Just the head, set perpendicular, bobbing with his breathing like a ball on water. He stepped out of sight, waited, stepped back into sight. The policeman's head withdrew, then re-emerged. His fringe. He did it again.

When Jesus was asked questions he didn't answer. Yes. Rarely. He would stop, and carry the question inside, like a doctor with a sick child. Time would open up a new room, and he would consider, and refer to things that had happened and had not yet happened, and to things that had been said and written down. And he would stare out of the window of this new room to see what it overlooked, and to measure the weather there, and the geography of the land, the grasses and the plants there, the animals in the foreground small and rustling, in the distance large and bellowing, so that all animals seemed the same size and to make the same noise. And he would wait. And sometimes he slept, or found himself reading, and he would forget that an answer was awaited, or he would pretend that he had forgotten. Eventually, slowly, with his voice, he would come out of the room with a healthy child. And he would provide his audience with something that was not an answer, but was instead a reflection and expansion of the question, a puzzle, something they could wander in and feel a sense of where he had been, and of what there was just out of their sight but within their reach.

He fumbled in his pockets. In full view. Patting his pockets. He pulled out a box of cigarettes, lit one. Dropped out of sight again. As if he was just pacing. To and fro. Came back. The policeman's head was all he could see. Respecting his wishes. He did it again. Out of sight. A different pause. Back in sight.

Then he went out of sight, threw away the cigarette and ran, faster than before, up the old path towards Highgate, by the backs of people's houses.

He was by instinct cruel.

He sat one afternoon in a café in a covered market. By the window, looking out at the stalls. Where was his wife? Cruising the knick-knack tables, examining the junk like diamonds, haggling with smelly little men over two quid off a matching choirboy and choirgirl, or a dog wearing a hat, or Churchill clutching his lapel. The high roof of the place let the cold air circulate and nothing heated it, and it felt like outdoors but it was covered and dry and the rain was kept out and he didn't give a shit about his wife any more. He didn't. He half hated her. He looked up from his soup and saw a woman looking in, wondering about a coffee maybe, a quick sandwich, a treat. Nice woman. She held an open umbrella over her head. He stared at her. And his eyes glanced up at the roof, and she saw him, and realized what she was doing, and laughed. She laughed, shook her head, *what am I like?* and lowered the umbrella. He could have smiled. He could have smiled and shook his head back at her – *what are you like?* or smiled and shrugged – *what are we all like, sometimes, sister?* or laughed aloud, kindly. Any of these things would be like a touch. A simple human touch. But he did none of these things. He stared at her. He stared and moved his hand slowly between the plate and his mouth. He stared and closed his

225

face, and made himself as a wall, and he said aloud the words *dumb bitch*, and her smile faltered and broke on the stones and she hesitated and was ashamed and she turned and walked away. And when she was gone he smiled. And he tried to tell himself that he had no access to time, and that his smile had simply come too late, that he was awkward and troubled and it wasn't his fault, that he was socially disadvantaged and that he was alienated from the community of ordinary people, and that it wasn't his fault.

But the truth was cruelty.

He needed someone to talk to.

Between the houses and the roofs the sky was black and purple, and past its edge was an egg yolk strip of the last of the sun, but at his feet there was darkness and around his body gloom, and nothing bright. The bushes came and went. There were some walkers. Things like that. He shouted. He looked into the gardens.

She would be on her second Coca-Cola. She said the sugar-free wouldn't hurt her. She would be watching *Millionaire* and wondering where he was.

There were windows lit. He saw a family in front of a television. He saw a couple cooking in a kitchen. Sirens behind him. Somewhere. He glimpsed lights. More sirens further away. He left the path, moved to his right, through grass and then a tangle of bushes and small trees down the embankment. He stumbled on a sharp decline, let himself slide on his arse and was poked in the face by a branch. He had to rip his way through the thickest of it, and came eventually to a wooden fence, the top coiled with wire. He turned and kicked at the middle with his right foot like a horse. It gave on the fifth. He turned again and made the hole usable and peered through it. A long garden. A kids' swing and slide set, cheap. A light in an upstairs window. Downstairs nothing, but the doors to the living room were glass. He climbed through the fence and sprinted towards them. Something moved in the window, upstairs. He swerved. He jumped the little flowerpots to the patio. He glimpsed a cartoon face on the floor – a T-shirt or a toy or something, staring at him. He got to the doors. Locked. He turned and kicked once and a panel shattered neatly. He squeezed through sideways and cut his stomach. Why hadn't he reached through and opened it? Why was he so stupid? He walked fast. He needed to get out of the room. He tripped on a low table and nearly fell. There were feet on the stairs, running. He found a door, opened it. A hallway. Light. There was a boy at the front door, leaving, struggling with the locks. He was about fifteen. Long hair.

– Stop. Wait. Please.

The boy looked back.

– Fuck.

He looked scared. Childish scared. His face wrinkled by bad-dream fear.

– No, please, wait.

The boy opened the front door and ran out. He ran on to

the road. T-shirt, long shorts, trainers. Then he stopped dead. In the middle of the road. And turned around.

– Come back. I won't hurt you. I can tell you things. We can talk. I have things no one else knows. No one at all. Ever. Come back.

The boy stepped further away. He looked like he might be crying. What was wrong with him?

– Come on, man. I will not hurt you.

The boy walked backwards, staring at him, until he bumped into a parked car. He ran around it, got it between them, put his hands on the roof. Circumauto.

– I want to have a conversation with you. That's all. Tell you some things. Then it's over. I promise. I promise you.

There was a siren. To his left. A squad car turned the corner. It braked a couple of houses away from him. A light came on and shone in his face. Nothing happened. He looked for the boy. He was gone. More sirens. Another car, unmarked. The sky was dark. There was nothing left on it.

He stepped back into the house and closed the door.

Jesus took a knife from his sandal. From the straps down there somehow. Where he had a sheath, a little leather knife holder. So. He took the knife from its place at his ankle, and he rose to his full height with the knife in a chisel grip. In his mind Jesus saw mouths talking, eating, sharing food. He saw an embrace, a handshake, a delicate murmured negotiation, an understanding, all the rooms opened up and the life of this man made brighter, wider, more interesting. And yet. There was so much time. Jesus brought his knife down the man's torso, splitting his cloth and his skin and his muscles and notching his ribs like a stick run down a wicker basket. And the blood clung to Jesus.

He imagined Jesus at this age. Early twenties. Rough as a branch, tall as a tree. His naked body in the river, laughing, watched and content to be watched. He imagined his voice raised to his mother. His fist raised to his father. His disappearances, for days. He imagined him fucking the strongest of women, hinting at kingdoms, showing them visions and miracles, attending to wants they did not know they carried. What is a blank time for, after all? What is the point of lost years if not to fill them with losses? He imagined Jesus standing over the flayed, shock-shouting man, and deciding in his amplitude of time to urinate on the wound and to laugh at the sadness he provoked in the strangest room of all.

Because this is human.

Jesus was a bastard. In the dark pit of his fear he carried the hope that for a while, Jesus was a bastard. An intolerant fucker, good with a knife.

He closed curtains, pulled down blinds, closed windows. He dragged a sofa from the living room and pulled it halfway up the stairs and jammed it there and something in his shoulder ripped. He went into the boy's room and switched off the light. A computer game was still running. He pulled out the plug. He went to the bathroom and pissed and flushed and washed his hands. The gloom was dense. He could hear sirens. All distant, none close. He could hear cars. The curtains in the large bedroom at the front were already closed. He crawled across the floor and kneeled and peeked through. There was a jumble of cars. Lights. There were people being ushered out of houses either side of him. They were getting organized.

He sat slouched with his back to the wall. Parents' bedroom. Cluttered. He could be tired if he wanted. It was all there. He could climb on to that bed and be asleep in five minutes. He would dream of the desert and the water and of walking and running. He could disappear into what he knew, what he'd thought of. No one would follow him.

There was a noise.

He tensed and stopped breathing.

Like a clopping sort of gurgle. Tiny. He looked at the door. Nothing. He would have heard. He looked at the ceiling. He'd only been in the house five minutes. Ten. No.

It came again.

There was a . . . thing, at the end of the bed. Like a box sitting on a table.

The boy had stopped and turned because he had remembered.

He stood up, then ducked. He crouched his way across the carpet and looked in the crib. It was not what he wanted. The baby was months old. It stared at him and didn't seem to mind. There was a smell. It needed changing.

– Hello?

He threw himself to the floor. It came from downstairs.

– Anyone home? Moss? Moss? I'm not armed, Moss! I'm on my own. There's a baby upstairs. Front bedroom. I just want to get her out, OK? Nothing else. So don't fucking shoot me.

He was in the living room. He'd come through the back garden. The way Moss had come. How did he know his name? He couldn't watch the front and back at the same time. He hadn't watched anything. He couldn't do this and that. He couldn't. Jesus. Babies, and men who knew his name.

– Moss? You hear me? You still here?

– Who are you?

– Child. My name is Child. You know me.

No he didn't.

– No I don't. Child?

– Yeah you do. I arrested you last year at your flat. Remember? You had that fight with your neighbour.

He remembered a van full of cops. His wife screaming in the stairwell. He didn't want to remember it. He stood up. Moved away from the baby. She was awake and she didn't seem to mind anything.

– I don't remember you.

– Yeah you do. We had a talk about the noise yeah? About your neighbour. About going to the council. Doing it right. You got it sorted, yeah? All that.

Glasses. Raincoat. And his partner, a skinny white man with a grin.

– Oh yeah.

– OK.

He was in the hallway.

– You find the baby, Moss?

– She need . . . she need a change.

– Just hand her down to me, will you, Moss? Then I'll be out of your way.

Saying his name all the time.

– No, man. Can't do that.

Why not?

– Oh come on, Moss. Seriously. They did like a morning of hostage negotiation training and I was fucking hung-over man, you know?

– How did you get here?

– I drove.

– Where did you fucking come from? I've been here like ten minutes.

– We saw you running. We were coming out of the Transport Police. Finsbury Park bus station. You went past like Usain fucking Bolt, Moss. P.C. after you.

He was calm. Relaxed. His voice. He was even cheerful. Moss wiped his forehead and looked at the crib.

– Then you were all over the radio. So we came up this way. Someone saw you getting through the fence. Neighbour. Road will be sealed off by now. Major incident shit. Congratulations.

– Why did you come in here?

– To get the baby.

– Just like that? I could have shot you.

He moved towards the bedroom door. Stuck his head out and pulled it back. He couldn't see down the stairs. He edged out.

– Well, yeah. There's a hysterical kid out there who left without his sister. It was either me come in or him, and the way he's carrying on I wouldn't really blame you if you shot him.

– He forgot her.

– It happens.

– He OK?

There was a pause.

– Yeah. So, now. You going to help me? I talked to you before. I know you're reasonable, Moss. You let me walk out of here with a baby in my arms I'm the fucking hero, you know? I'll get a medal out of it.

He could see just shapes in the darkness. Shadows and other shadows.

– If there's reward money I'll split it with you.

He could see the glow of light from the street. He could see maybe the top of his head. The sofa was blocking the view.

– Move back a bit so I can see you. Stand by the front door.

He did it. He was tall.

– Turn on a light.

– Yeah?

– Yeah. I want to see you.

They would wait. They would wait until this guy walked

out with the baby or without the baby. He wouldn't walk out without the baby.

– I have a gun on you.

– Yeah.

A shadow changed shape as he reached out. He was groping along the wall.

– Can't find it. Oh.

Click. He squinted, Child did. They both did. One arm out to the light switch, the other raised as well, palm forward. He wore a stab vest over a T-shirt. One of the fasteners, under his left arm, was loose. He wore jeans. His glasses were halfway down his nose. He was tall and looked strong.

– You remember me?

Moss kept his body hidden. He was behind the sofa, behind banisters, at an angle, out of the light.

– I remember you.

– Not armed, see? Pockets are empty.

He turned slowly in a circle.

– I just want the baby, and I'm out of here.

– I need to keep her.

Child looked at him with a sort of grimace.

– Why? Why would you want to do that?

– You send the boy back in and I'll let you have the baby.

Child raised his eyebrows. Gave a sort of smile.

– That's not going to happen, Moss.

– Well that's it, man. Either the baby or the boy. That's fucking it.

*

Jesus sipped wine and watched the door and wondered why the old man in the corner of the room was so worried. He had learned, over the years, to close people off from his mind. He had become like others. People sat by him now and noticed nothing odd. They felt no strange consciousness wandering their own; they did not feel suddenly understood. They rarely experienced the alarm of realizing, mid-thought, that they were overheard. He could see that the man was worried.

– What troubles you, Father?

And even still the old man seemed surprised. He peered into Jesus's gloomy corner and licked his lips and squinted to see and stood and took up his cup and came over, limping.

– Who are you?

– Jesus of Nazareth.

The man's eyes strained and he shook his head.

– I am fucked, my brother. My wife is dying. My son is ill and has no money. My leg is swollen. There is no god.

– There is a God.

– There is no god.

– No, really, there is. Look.

And Jesus showed him God.

– What about me? I take the baby out. I leave her on the doorstep even, and I come back in. You keep me.

– You're no good.

– She's quiet. She OK?

– She's fine. She's awake. She's just lying there.

– Why am I no good?

Moss touched the knife. These people. They covered the city with points. Dozens of points. Hundreds of points. Thousands, probably, of points. Millions of points. They covered the city with points. Each point wobbling in the new dark. There was a jelly over the city, and they had strings with which to section off and slice it.

Moss never tried to think of a modern Jesus, a Jesus today. Such a thing was beyond him. It was beyond everyone. Jesus would be a shock, a violent intervention, a calamity. He would fuck things up. He would terrify all settled minds, petrify the structures. Such a thing, as a man, could not be imagined. This is why people did not believe.

The baby cried. Once. Just a little half wail. Then a gurgle and a cough. Then another half cry or half laugh.

– When Jesus was a boy . . .

– What?

– When Jesus was a boy. There was trouble.

– Can I put my arms down?

– Yes.

– I'm not religious.

– A boy was found. By the river. He had been beaten. He had been badly beaten. A woman, who was a nurse, she found him. She had not even intended to go that way, but for some reason, when she was walking home after seeing a new mother, she turned to walk by the river. She found this boy.

About ten years old. Unconscious. Bleeding. His nose broken.
A rib cracked. Bruising. Very bad.

Child put his hands in his pockets. Moss held his eyes.

– Don't do that, man.

Child took his hands out of his pockets.

– Sorry.

– So she called some men, and they carried him home,
and the nurse tended to him and he was OK. He would be
OK. And when he woke up the men asked him what had
happened. He refused to say. He would not tell them who had
beaten him.

– Just let me take the baby, Moss. We have guys who are
trained for this sort of thing. You know, talking.

– I thought you wanted me to keep you?

He said nothing. He just nodded.

– Some of the men knew that this boy was a bully. The
beaten boy. They knew that he picked on others. They suspected that one of these boys' older brothers had perhaps
wanted to teach him a lesson. They asked around. They
learned that recently the beaten boy had been picking on
Jesus. Saying things about his mother.

– Moss.

– What?

– Do you even have a gun?

He said nothing. He turned his head and looked back
towards the baby.

– You won't read this story in the gospels.

– No?

– No. This is from the suppositions of the Association.

– The what?

– The suppositions of the Association.

– What association?

– The Association of Christ Sejunct.

– Saint John?

– Sejunct.

– Say junk?

– Sejunct.

– What's that?

– The Association of Christ Sejunct is an association of Earth-bound sinners who keep alive in our hearts and in our daily lives, with an honest strength and an honest weakness, the solemn consideration of the sublime figure of Jesus our Saviour and Balm, in the years during which he is separated from our knowledge of him – from his circumcision to the age, by the Gospel of Luke, of twelve, when he attends to and questions the teachers in the Temple, and from then until the beginning of his blessed ministry.

Child nodded. He was smiling.

– That's quite something, he said.

Moss nodded.

– Who is in the Association?

– I am. And my wife. And some others. And you, now, as well. You are in the Association.

– OK. I'm in it? How am I in it?

– Anyone who hears about the Association of Christ Sejunct is in the Association of Christ Sejunct. You will start to wonder. Now it's in you to wonder. You will wonder, and you will come to believe things. About what else happened. In all those years. The gap in the story.

– I'm not religious.

– Neither am I.

– Can I have the baby?

– Yes.

He didn't move.

– Do you have a gun?

He didn't answer.

– Do you know the people in this house?

He didn't answer.

– The boy. Do you know the boy?

He didn't answer.

– I have so many stories, he said. Turn off the light.

He used his lighter to see his way back to the child, and his fingers burned and when he put them to his mouth he tasted his own warm blood. She stared at the flame.

– Don't move, he shouted.

She jumped and her face crumpled and she started to cry.

– Shit. Not you – Child.

He grimaced. What a name for a man.

– I'm not moving, Moss. I haven't moved an inch.

– I'll shoot the baby.

239

– No you won't.

He pocketed his lighter. He pulled the knife out of his leg pocket and looked at it. If he stuck it in his waistband somehow it might look like the grip of a pistol. And it would cut him. He stuck the blade under his belt at his back, within reach of his right hand, the hilt holding it. He wondered for a second if there might be a toy gun in the boy's room. He pulled out his lighter again and looked around. The baby was crying steady, complaining. He was able to ignore her. He wondered if there was a length of time they gave Child before they decided that he was dead, and called the telephone or switched on a loudspeaker. He couldn't see a telephone. There was a hairbrush on the bedside table. What sort of mother leaves a newborn in the care of a kid playing computer games in another room?

The baby was soft and she cried more when he lifted her. Jesus had two younger brothers and two younger sisters. Something like that. He would watch them sleep, and carry them around, and sing to them. He liked to sing to them. When they were older they would try to make him sing to them again. But he became embarrassed for a while and would not sing. And then song became something else that he did not do. He had put so much behind him by the time he started.

– Sshhh sshhh little girl. You're OK.

He carried her to the door.

– Have you moved?

– Not an inch.

– I'm coming out. I'm armed.

– Yeah. No problem. Take it easy.

He opened the door wider with his foot and shuffled through it. Child's silhouette was as he'd left it, standing on the stairs with its hands laid flat on the upturned back of the sofa. All the dark seemed to fill with little ghosts. A flickering blue glow came from the street.

– You made her cry.

– Lift your hands. Both hands. You hold her with both hands, OK?

Child nodded with the glow behind him, nothing like a halo. The baby stopped crying and listened, and Moss held her out. Child's glasses shot sparks, and the muscles of Moss's arms ached in the quiet. The city was never like this. He paused. He stopped. He held her in mid-air.

– What?

– If I give her to you what will happen?

– I told you. I take her out. I hand her over to her mother.

– What will happen to me?

– You have a phone?

– No.

– Well. I don't know. The negotiating guys will arrive. They'll send in a phone or something. You can talk with them. Demand a flight to Cuba. Or a pizza. Whatever.

He withdrew her. She gurgled. She smelled awful. He would have to change her, feed her. They would wonder about that. Him and the baby. Not him only, but him and the baby.

– Come on, Moss. You give me the baby and I'll tell them you have a gun.

His face was a shadow.

– What?

– I'll tell them you have a gun. It's what you want, isn't it? Big siege. Days, maybe. Centre of attention. With a bit of luck you'll get shot. And you'll be the people's hero and we'll look like trigger-happy shits again.

It was Jesus who had beaten the boy. But he said nothing. He said nothing because he knew that there was nothing to be made of it. Of what had happened. That it had simply happened. He loved his mother, and he knew that he would cause her grief, unbearable grief, and he wished to protect her, and cause her only joy. And he knew the boy was just a boy, saying foolish things that were not true, and that the insult really was not against his mother but against him, that it was a test, an exploration of his strength, as these things are measured amongst boys. And he knew that though he could kill the boy with a thought, he did not want to kill anyone with a thought. And that the boy would love him if he beat him and was fair in the beating. So he beat him. And he was fair in the beating. And the boy loved him and was changed. Later, when he was older, Jesus would experiment with unfairness, with cruelty. But as this age, he was fair.

He held her out again. She gurgled in his arms. Her tiny

fingers stretched and grasped in the half light like an upturned insect. He held her out. He couldn't see Child's hands. He thought he could see Child's hands. He tipped the baby forward, rolled her, almost, and Child said something, and the baby seemed to be taken, and his hands were empty and she was gone, and Child shouted something, and something fell, and there was movement, a blur of it, and a small white shape seemed to bounce off the upturned edge of the sofa, and roll or trickle to the right, over the banister, and down through the panicking ghosts to the floor of the hall, where it stopped with a split thump like a punch.

There was silence. Nothing. The bundle didn't move.

– Jesus fucking Christ.

Child turned on the stairs and tumbled down and wheeled and was at her side, on his knees, fumbling.

– Jesus fucking Christ, he said.

Then he said nothing else.

All the dark looked up at Moss. Jesus is appalled by man.

– Child?

Child stood and seemed to take his time going to the light switch and snapping it on. The ghosts all scattered and the dark was gone. The baby lay broken.

There was a gap.

The Referee

They came out through the smallest darkness, a night that lasted nothing, and Child moaned into the cold about sleep and his dreams, and Hawthorn hummed for warmth and thought about men, various men, whom he moved about his mind like furniture.

Rivers talked to them in a corridor. A conversation Hawthorn would have preferred to have sitting down, over a coffee. With a little back and forth perhaps. A little teasing out of options. There was too much in it. His legs hurt. He scribbled in his notebook, scratched his eyebrows with the pen, brushed crumbs from his jacket, looked at his boss's lapels. Rivers wasn't doing options. It was probably some sort of management thing – talking to them in a noisy corridor, getting in people's way.

– And drop by Johnson at some stage and get the sheets from those last couple of weeks. October. We need to get the story straight on that Rafsan thing.

Hawthorn glanced at Child. He was nodding.

Johnson. Sheets. Rafsan.

– And Mishazzo is your priority then. After that. We need

to do it or drop it, and I'm not dropping it. So clear this crap today and then it's Mishazzo to the end.

People were brushing past them. Someone knocked his elbow, apologized. Rivers leaned a hand on the wall and lifted a foot and did something with his sock. They were about fifteen feet from his empty office. Hawthorn's fingers were stiff. His writing looked ridiculous.

– Thank you, gentlemen.

– Sir.

Child flung the car around and Hawthorn dozed. He thought about his father and his brother. He thought about the empty floor of his kitchen and the window that looked over roofs. He remembered or imagined, he couldn't tell, certain sexual scenes. He looked at the doorways, then the sky. He mumbled.

– What?

– Nothing. Rivers annoys me.

Child grunted.

– He's mostly bullshit.

– We're all mostly bullshit.

Hawthorn yawned.

– Are we.

– We are.

They were out of their usual area. Hawthorn couldn't remember why. He went rummaging for his notebook.

– What was all that, talking to us in the fucking corridor?

– He likes to look busy.

– And, said Child, this is Mickey Mouse, this is. Rafsan, for fuck's sake.

Hawthorn was trying to read street signs, and his notebook.

– Where are we? Who the fuck is Rafsan?

– I think he's over it though. You losing the driver kid. He's decided to leave it. He has to make something happen with Mishazzo now, you know? He's leaning that way. You think?

– I didn't lose the driver. Who is Rafsan?

Child laughed.

– Oh, Hawthorn. You are a terrible fucking detective.

– *Johnson. Sheets. Rafsan.* What the fuck is that? And where the fuck are we?

– Copenhagen in the springtime.

They were on Waterloo Bridge.

– What are we doing down here?

– You keep the worst notes ever. And because you write things down you think you've understood them. And remembered them. And you haven't. You've just scribbled some random fucking words and your brain has neglected to retain any single piece of information it's received.

Hawthorn grunted. Child opened the window.

– The film place, remember? The guy in the film place.

– Right.

He thought of his father. His father would run a bath with hot water only, then let it cool down. He refused to run cold water. He liked a steamy bathroom, he said. Stupid.

– What guy in what film place?

＊

– You see dead people?

– Among others. Yes.

– Like the movie?

– I'm not dead.

– No. No, you're not dead. You're the kid in the movie. I'd be the dead one. If we're talking about the movie. I'm Bruce Willis. You're the boy. What do you mean, *among others?*

– I see people who are alive as well.

– Like me?

– No. People who aren't there. Or . . . older versions of people. I mean younger versions of them. I see my mother sometimes. She's alive. She's nearly seventy. When I see her she's my age. Or younger.

– How do you know it's her?

– I know my own mother.

– These are the emails. There are twelve. The last one arrived yesterday, after I talked to you. Or your colleague.

He handed Hawthorn some print-outs.

– When was the first one?

– About two weeks ago.

– So they've been coming in pretty regularly.

– Every couple of days.

Hawthorn read one of them.

Dear Fillfuck FakePEDO

Ur scum and I let them know u are.U pedo pervert.I will kill you

and noone will care.Cos you are a pedo. D.I.E .. .U fucke I

have pictures.

Real Man

He handed it to Child and glanced through the others.

– We'll need the long headers on these, he said.

– The what?

– At the top there. It gives the email address, but the system also gets the I.P. address. Which gives us the location of the computer it was sent from.

He looked blank.

– Your IT guys will do it for us.

– I haven't told anyone here. Except my boss.

– OK. Well, we can be discreet about it. But it's important that we get that information.

– OK.

He was about thirty. Skinny. He seemed very worried.

– You have no idea who this might be?

– No.

– Just to your work address?

– Yes.

– Nothing odd showing up on your Facebook or in chat or any other websites or anything?

– Nothing at all.

– You went to Poland?

– To a film festival, yes.

– He has that?

– Yes, he mentions it in one of them.

Child read it out.

– *Did you like the polish girls you raped? You like them 12 and 13? I'm fucking watching you.*

Child had his glasses perched on the top of his head. Hawthorn stared at him. He'd never seen that before. Child took the glasses down and put them back on to look at the guy.

– Who knew you were going to Poland?

– Well. Anyone here, obviously. I mentioned it to some friends. It's not like it was a secret or anything.

Child did the thing with the glasses again. Sitting them on top of his head like sunglasses. Hawthorn smiled.

– He sort of bangs on about the paedophile thing, Child said.

Hawthorn looked back at the guy. Phil.

– I'm not a paedophile.

– Why would he say that?

– Because it's a horrible thing to say?

Child nodded.

– So you have no idea who this might be?

– None at all. Really none. I have tried to work it out. But I can't. I don't know.

– Are you involved in politics at all?

– No.

– Do you own property?

250

– No, I rent. Why?

– Not involved in any legal disputes or litigation of any sort?

– No, nothing.

– Do you have a relative who might be involved in anything like that? Any sort of dispute?

– Nothing I know about.

– Any ex-girlfriends or boyfriends you think might get into something like this?

– No.

– You're sure.

– Yes. Completely sure.

– So you have no names to give us? To check out? No suspicions about anyone?

– You're making me feel like it's my fault that I don't know who it is. I just don't know. I haven't the faintest idea.

Child nodded.

– OK. Thanks. If you could point us towards your IT guys. And we'll get back to you when we know something.

They spent another hour there. Hawthorn wrote a lot of notes. It was warm in the building. He liked the cinema smell. As they were leaving he grabbed a programme for the LGBT Film Festival. Child rolled his eyes.

– Don't leave that in my fucking car.

– It's not your fucking car.

– You want to drive?

– What's this thing with your glasses?

– What thing?

– Putting them on top of your head when you read.

– I read better without my glasses.

– How does that work?

– I don't fucking know. It's getting more and more difficult to read things with my glasses on.

– Maybe I should drive.

– It's not my distance vision. That hasn't changed. I just can't fucking read with my glasses and I can't see any distance without them. I'm getting fucking old.

– Yeah.

– You can't drive.

– I can drive.

– No you can't. He's a paedo, you know.

– Who?

– That guy. Phil.

– You think?

– He is. I tell you. I bet fifty quid if we grabbed his home computer we'd get a stash of little girl pics. Bet you these I.P. addresses are from a bunch of Internet cafés within oozing distance of an RSO or three.

– In London, said Hawthorn.

– You are never more than nine feet away, said Child.

– From a registered sex offender, they said, together.

– What do they say?

– Not a lot.

– You see them all the time?

– No. Maybe once or twice a day.

– All your life?

– I think so. There was a time in my teens that I thought I'd stopped seeing them. But I think I just ignored them for a couple of years.

They lay on the bed in sunlight, looking out over the East End.

– Do you see them when you're with other people?

– Yeah. I can see them any time.

– You see any now?

He glanced around the room. He looked out of the window.

– You see that building over to the left? The smaller one. With the balconies.

– Yeah.

– So, three floors down from the top, the centre balcony?

– Yeah.

– You see anyone there?

– No.

He smiled.

– Then I see one now.

They went to a hanging in Kentish Town.

Something odd about it. On the radio.

– This is the third this month.

– Fourth.

– Fourth this month.

Frank Lenton called.

– Rivers, he said.

– What about him?

– He knows this woman. Knew this woman. He turned up out of the blue when there was just Lowry and Chudasama there. Barged in and practically collapsed. He must have heard the address on the radio. He's completely out of it. Lowry and Chuds had to take him back here, then home. So. You know. Sensitivity.

Child and Hawthorn looked at each other.

– What do you want us to do?

– Well. Nothing. The usual.

– Nothing different then?

– Nothing.

– Right.

It smelled horrible. From the front door they got a wave of barbecue and shit. They glanced at each other. They pulled on gloves. They pulled on shoe-bags. In the hallway it was a burned Sunday roast and something sharp like plastic. The uniforms weren't happy. Forensics were there, hanging around, waiting. They didn't look happy either.

It was a large three-storey house with a big basement kitchen. It was nice. Roomy, full of light. Recently redecorated. By the sink, over the cooker, beside the window to the back garden, something hung improbably, a bit like a deflated balloon.

They stared at it. A uniform stood in the doorway and told them various facts, which they applied to what they saw in front of them with limited success.

She was called Misha Palmer. At least they assumed that's who it was. They'd no reason to believe it was anyone else. She was in her mid-forties. She shared with four other tenants. She had waited for everyone to go to work. Then she had gone to the kitchen, taken off her nightdress, which now lay crumpled in the sink, dismantled and removed the extractor hood over the cooker, attached a rope somehow to the wall, had fixed the other end around her neck, lit the rings on the gas hob, and she had knelt forward from the back wall, over the flames, asphyxiating herself as her flesh burned.

There was no note, the uniform told them.

Hawthorn went to throw up in the back garden and found the spot everyone else had used. That didn't help. Child lasted another few minutes and then did the same.

– She has to hate her life.

– She has to hate herself.

– Yeah.

– I mean really, really *hate* herself.

– Yeah.

The uniform followed them. Giving them facts. The fire alarm and the smoke through the window brought neighbours, and the fire brigade, and firemen had broken in the front door and found her.

– They spray her with anything?

– Yeah.

– What?

– I don't know.

– Why haven't they moved her?

– No one has signed off on it yet. The other detectives left, to . . .

– OK, OK. What have forensics done?

– Everything except the body. And by the body. Around the body.

Hawthorn looked at the kitchen window. It was blackened, like a bucket of paint had been flung over the corner near the cooker. Cracks had appeared. There was a hole punched through the top corner. The bricks above it glistened. He walked over. There was something . . . a cable, running through the extractor fan hole and tight across the wall, and back in through the corner of the window.

– Look. Look what she's done.

Child came over. They stood there. They stood there studying the cable for a long time, and Child shared his mints with Hawthorn, and Hawthorn gave Child a clean tissue.

They went back inside.

Hawthorn looked at her. It took a moment to work out which way she was facing, and that the smudged thumbprint on her head was the remains of her face. Her legs were no longer discrete limbs but had merged into something very like a cheap Christmas candle, melted, and it took him a while to recognize the glint in the red wax as exposed bone. The smell was baked sweet.

People watched them. Hawthorn didn't know what to do.

Child stepped closer to her. He held his nose and looked carefully where he put his feet. The cooker and the floor in front of it were covered in a layer of fat and foam.

– Where are her hands?

Hawthorn took a step. He stopped. He didn't know where her hands were.

– There, he said.

– Where?

– There. At the end of her arms.

Child turned and stared at him. Then he turned back.

– Oh yeah, he said.

They moved around her like she might attack them.

– I don't see how she did it.

– There was a chair, someone said.

– What?

– One of the chairs was up against the counter.

– OK. She climbs on a chair. And on to the counter. She detaches the hood. That exposes the hole in the wall I suppose. She drops the hood and all that crap over there.

– OK.

– There's glass on the window sill. On the inside I mean. So. She feeds the cable through the extractor hole, climbs back down, goes out to the garden, breaks the window with something. Stick or something. Her fist maybe . . . and gets the cable and feeds it back through there. Comes back in, ties it off, loops it . . . I can't see the knot. Then she lights the hob. This all been photographed?

– Yes, sir.

Child stepped up to the counter. Hawthorn watched his bagged feet. They slid slightly.

– How does she light the hob while she's hanging?

– She lights, then hangs.

– How does she do that? She'd be burning.

– She's going to be burning anyway. What does she care?

Child coughed. He was peering behind her. He coughed again.

– OK.

He looked down at his feet. Hawthorn looked as well. Child moved one a little. It squirmed. There are ghosts sometimes, Hawthorn thought, and that's all. Just ghosts. And they come out of the past and they stare at us and then they disappear. And that's all that happens. He looked at her face. It wasn't really there. He looked at her body. She looked mostly like a spill of paint. Or a pencil drawing started, then erased. He supposed that was what she wanted.

– Fuck, said Child. OK. This is not a crime scene.

He was in front of the television, crying. He didn't know what he was crying about. He was naked. He looked at his phone. There were two missed calls. One from his brother and one from the referee. He had fallen asleep. It had been hot but it was cold now. He went and got his dressing gown from the bathroom and sat down again in front of the television and stopped himself from crying with tissues and a thinking strategy. It involved calling to mind simple everyday generic things and visualising them in detail. A cup and saucer. A bus. A carton of milk. Blank things. He turned off the television. He didn't know what to do.

– What if they're not real ghosts?

   – What do you mean?

   – I mean. If they're not real. You know. You're just imagining them.

He pulled Hawthorn's head around to face him and held it there.

   – They're just in my mind?

   – Yes.

He stuck his finger in Hawthorn's mouth. Two fingers. He held his hair.

   – What's the difference? Eh? What. Is. The. Fucking. Difference.

They took her down. The coroner's people. Parts of her adhered to the cooking surface, to the counter top. They laid a body bag on the draining board. They didn't quite know how to proceed. They came and went, making phone calls. Hawthorn and Child looked around the house. In her room there were posters of kittens and sunsets and maps of South

America and photographs of her – they assumed – in famous places. There was one of her and a younger Rivers at a picnic table, laughing, their shoulders together, staring wide-eyed at the camera as if the joke came from there. There were books on Atlantis and the Incas and the Amazon and the Lost Tribes of the Rainforest. She had made her bed. The duvet neatly folded back, the pillows puffed up, a teddy bear with a red bow tie propped in the corner. The window was open. Child went through drawers. Hawthorn wandered back downstairs. She was still there. Still slumped on the worktop like a failed cake.

There was a gap in the coming and going. Hawthorn was alone with her. He took out his phone and took some photographs. Seven. He took seven photographs.

Hawthorn and Child leaned against each other near the open door of the bookies, but not so as you'd notice.

– Tall guy, clumsy, bit like that you know. Came in looking for his dog. Said he had a dog. Lost dog. So I says to him there ain't no dog in here mate, is there? But he's looking around, you know, looking under the chairs, shifting people out of the way, swinging around suddenly like it might be behind him, and I'm like, *oi-oi, we got a right one here*, and I'm about to go and show him the door when he comes up to the counter and wants to go back there to look for his bloody dog. And I can see in his eyes he's a bit of a loon, you know, and I get a flash of the fear and all. Just a flash. Like, this one isn't right. We get loons in here all the live-long day it's not a problem, is it? Regulars, most of them. Put a one-quid bet on horses with colours in their names, or they do that numbers thing, that Muslim stuff, sorry mate I don't know what you call it, that numbers and colours and all that shit. They don't bother anyone. Well, they bother some, but they're harmless, you know, just the mumbles and the plastic bags and the odd bit of crazy shouting at the telly during a race, that's all right. This one though. Had that stare. You know it. I didn't like it one bit. So I try to humour him. I stand back so he can see in, so he can look at the floor, and I tell him, no dog in here mate, look, can you see a dog, I'd have seen a dog, I been in here all morning, and he's standing there looking at me, and his hands are on the counter, you know, and he's clenching his fists. Clenching and unclenching. And he's looking more and more desperate. Like he knows as well, same as I know, that he's not right, and he doesn't want it to happen any more than I do. So I ask him, what's the dog's name. And he stares at me. Mouth open, surprised I think he was, and I'm like, oh that's good – I've engaged him, you know, he sees me now. But he just stares, so I ask him again, what's the dog's name, mate, and he says, I don't fucking know, he says it quiet like that, but then he starts shouting, I don't fucking know what the fucking dog's fucking name is, how the fuck would I know the fucking name of the fucking dog, and I know I'm in trouble then, 'cos he has the rage on him. Complete rage. I ain't never seen anything like it. And he punches the glass. Once. Twice. And

I nod at Alice to hit the alarm button, and on the third punch I'm pretty sure I see him break bones, and on the fourth or fifth he's got a crack along the whole window, so he picks up the chair and hammers at it and it smashes like a useless bit of crap, and he's through there before I know what the hell is going on, and the rest is a bit of a blur to be honest. Bit of a blur. Alice's nose is broken they tell me, and there are a couple of loose teeth. But she'll live.

– So who is it?

– Who is what?

– The bloke.

– What bloke?

Child put his feet up on the chair opposite him and slumped. He sucked his coffee and made a face.

– There's a way you go.

– What way?

– You get all thinky. Extra stupid. You go from being a bad detective to being a stupid one.

– Cheers.

– I'd call it love in someone else. But I know you. You're incapable of love.

– Yeah.

– You are capable only of worry and violence.

– He's a referee.

Child turned briefly and looked at him.

– A referee. A football referee?

– A football referee. Premiership.

– Fuck off.

– No. Seriously. Does internationals.

– Fuck off.

– Not internationals. What do I mean? Club internationals.

– European?

– European, yeah. Italy, Spain, Germany. He was in . . . I can't tell you, can I? 'Cos you'll look it up and out him for five hundred quid to the fucking *Sun* or something.

– You can tell me anything.

– He's a seriously strange man. Not strange. Fucked up. Maybe fucked up. Maybe just strange.

– What matches has he done? Name some clubs.

– He's done them all. He's, you know, one of the top ones. One of the top referees in Europe. He does the big games.

– You have no idea.

– He was in Frankfurt last week. Next week he's in Italy. This weekend he's not doing a premiership match, he's doing some other thing.

– It's a cup weekend. Frankfurt?

– Some youth thing, that was. He said. Germany and Spain or something. That was an international, but a youth one.

– He told you this? What age is he?

– He has photos of players on his walls. Photos of him shaking hands with captains. You know, Van Persie . . . Vidic, John Terry. All those guys. He's . . .

– He can get you tickets, then.

– What?

– Tickets for games.

Hawthorn rolled his shoulder and hummed.

– When do I get to meet him?

Hawthorn shook his head.

– Is he out?

– No. Very not out.

– How did you meet him?

– Online. He believes in ghosts.

– He believes in ghosts.

– He says he sees them all the time. You know. In his home. On the pitch. In his car. In airplanes . . .

– On the pitch?

– On the pitch.

– During games? On the pitch during games?

– Yeah.

– He sees ghosts?

– Yeah.

Child laughed.

– I want a cigarette.

Child said nothing. Coughed a bit, artificially. Indicated left. Turned left.

– Me too, he said.

They drove for a while, the radio crackling. Hawthorn poked text into his phone.

– Why is that?

– Cigarettes?

– Yeah.

– It's an afterwards thing. A taste-smell thing. Back of the throat. Roof of the mouth. Mints don't get to it.

He turned on to the Holloway Road. Traffic was stopped. He pulled in behind a bus advertising tanning lotion straight at them, the ad the size of their windscreen. Hawthorn tried not to read it. Looked at his phone.

– No note.

– No note.

– The way she did it speaks volumes.

– To who? The firemen? Us?

Hawthorn thought maybe the smell had crept into the car on their clothes. In their hair.

– When was the last time you had a cigarette?

Child hummed.

– A straight-up fag? I don't know. Years. Six fucking years or something. You?

– Three or four.

Hawthorn looked at the pavement. A woman was standing outside a shop, smoking. Looking at him.

– I really want one.

– Get some.

– What?

– Hop out. Get a pack.

He laughed.

– Of what?

– Cigarettes, you fucking numpty.

– What brand?

– I don't fucking know.

Hawthorn opened the door. He was still wearing his seat belt. The bus moved on.

– Shit. Hang on.

Child pulled up on the kerb. The cars behind started blowing horns. Hawthorn undid his seat belt. Opened the door properly.

– Not Silk Cut. Don't get Silk Cut. I hate Silk Cut.

– They don't even make Silk Cut any more.

– They don't?

– Not in years, man.

He had no idea if this was true. He slammed the door and the horns beeped at him. He glanced back to see Child stick the light on the roof and turn it on, silently. The horns stopped, the nearest first and then backwards in a wave.

They still made Silk Cut. He felt like a schoolboy. He bought a packet of ten Benson & Hedges. He couldn't believe how much they cost.

They pulled in beside the Emirates and Hawthorn peeled the cellophane off and flipped the lid and slid the foil away from the filters packed tight, and Child watched him and they looked at each other and smiled and looked at their cigarettes.

– This is great.

– You got matches?

– No.

Child frowned and Hawthorn pulled a lighter from his pocket and Child smiled again. Bic. Black.

– You diamond.

– Open the windows.

Hawthorn pulled a couple, three, of the cigarettes proud of the pack and offered them to Child. He pulled one out fully, sniffed it like it was a cigar, and put it to his lips. Hawthorn took one for himself, and tapped the filter end a couple of times against the packet. Child laughed.

– You so classy.

Hawthorn threw the packet on the dashboard. He put the cigarette in his mouth. He held the lighter in both hands. He scraped his thumb on the wheel, once, twice, and sparks flew and died in front of him, and on the third a nipple of flame pulsed and grew and steadied, and he bowed the tip of his cigarette to the fire and sucked, gently, as precisely as he could, for a moment only, and he released his thumb and pulled his head back and let his mouth empty and a billow of smoke filled the air in front of him and he was smoking.

Child laughed again and took the lighter and lit his own.

They sat there saying nothing for a minute.

– So.

– So.

– Rivers, eh?

– Yeah.

– Ex, do you think?

– Nah. Hardly. You think so?

Hawthorn took another drag. Slightly too much. Child was experimenting with his hold. He looked awkward when he transferred it from one hand to the other.

– I don't know. We'll find out. No doubt.

– It's gotta rankle. Either way.

– It's gotta what?

– Rankle.

– Rankle?

– Seeing someone you know. Who's done that to themselves.

– It *rankles*?

– Yeah. Rankles. What's wrong with you?

– I don't think *rankle* is the word you're looking for.

– Well what is the word then?

A centimetre of ash fell on Hawthorn's thigh. He brushed at it, it left a mark.

– Horror. Horrifies. It would horrify me. Grief, shock, all that.

– Yeah, but anger too.

– Some anger. Why anger?

– It's quite a statement.

Child looked at him.

– Oh. Hey. I get it. You think she knew Rivers would be on scene.

Hawthorn shrugged. He felt a little dizzy.

– Well. She knows it's his patch I presume. Maybe she knows that he wasn't working yesterday but was today. Maybe she knows he'll hear about it, come running. I mean. Maybe she doesn't. Maybe it hasn't. Occurred to her. But . . .

Child laughed.

– Oh, you pulling a whitey.

– A what?

– You've gone white as a ghost, man. You've got a sheen on you. Clammy. Getting a touch of the queasies, yeah?

– Shut up.

– Do not throw up in my car.

– I'm not going to fucking throw up. And it's not your car.

– First time I smoked, I was about twelve or something, I got into it for a while, and my buddy Malcolm got into it too but he would throw up. Every time. He would take a couple of drags and he'd hurl. Every time. For months. Never got used to it. He looked like fucking death. His mother thought he had anorexia.

Hawthorn wanted to say something but his mouth had dried up. He took another drag of his cigarette, carefully, not inhaling.

– You should have got water. Oh. We have water. Here.

Hawthorn took it.

– So Malcolm, eventually he decided that smoking wasn't for him.

Hawthorn looked at the cigarette in his hand. It shook

slightly. He threw it out of the window. He felt sick and embarrassed. He wanted to belch. He sipped from the water bottle. Child was laughing at him now. But he wasn't smoking his either.

— This was a bad a idea.

— No it wasn't. It was a great idea. Great idea. Your best idea ever. You've got ash all over you.

It seems wrong. The door half open. The light on. It is mid-afternoon. He looks at the photographs on his phone. They aren't very good. If you didn't know what they were, you wouldn't know what they were. He puts it away. The light is on because no one is there. If there was someone there the light would not be on. The referee's left it on. Or one of his ghosts has left it on. And the door is open. But he only notices it's open because the light is on. He looks out of the window. Three floors from the top, middle balcony. He's there. But the light is still on. He's there but he shouldn't be. He doesn't know what to do, now that he's there. He doesn't care what might be in the drawers, the cupboards. He doesn't mind. He stands at the window. He has an erection and he presses it against the glass and tries to see the street but can't. The place should have an alarm system. He'll tell him. And the lock is useless. He'll tell him that too. Casually. As they're going out the door sometime, together. Community policing. He thinks about coming. On his clothes or into his laundry basket or the bar of soap in his shower. On his window. He goes to look in the bedroom. He remembers the angle of the open door before he changes it. The bed is made, neat. The duvet folded back. It's the bedside lamp that's been left on. There is no one in the room. Except Hawthorn. He thinks about getting into the bed. He doesn't. He doesn't want to. There is no one in the room. The made bed. He returns the door to the angle it was at. One third open and the light on.

There is no one anywhere.

He leaves.

– He sees ghosts.

– Yeah. He says they're just like people except they shimmer a little. They're half transparent. He can walk through them.

– Fuck's sake.

– He says he's always seen them.

– Arsehole.

– Except now he's worried, because he's starting to see them on the pitch. You know. During matches. They distract him.

– No shit.

– And he worries that they'll make him screw up or do something stupid.

– And you slept with this guy.

– Yeah.

– Was he seeing ghosts?

– Yeah.

– Oh for fuck's sake.

Hawthorn laughed.

– I need to hear this, said Child.

– Well I asked him what he was looking at. He was looking past me, you know.

– You're having sex?

– No, no. This was just sitting in his place. He pauses mid-sentence and looks past me. Over my shoulder. And I just glance back. You know. Behind me. He looks like he's seen something. But also like he's remembered something. I think he's remembered his dry cleaning or someone's birthday or something. And I look around in a half joking sort of way. You know. When someone does that pause, and stares off into space. And you look at where they're looking. Even though you know they're not actually looking at anything. I looked where he was looking, then turned back to him, and he stares at me as if I've done something weird. And I say *What*, and he says *Oh*. Just that. *Oh*. And he says, *for a second I thought you saw him too*.

– Oh my God.

– So then he just tells me that he sees ghosts. Or people. People I suppose. He assumes they're ghosts. Or, no. Hang on. He sees some people who aren't dead. But he sees previous versions of them. Including himself.

– This is not getting better.

– He sees, like, himself as a kid. Or he sees his mother as a young woman. Or his grandfather as a teenager. And he recognizes those people. He sees loads of people he doesn't recognize. He assumes they're the ghosts.

– And you stayed?

Hawthorn shrugged.

– Do they speak to him?

– No. He says that used to drive him mad. That he'd endlessly try to get them to talk to him. But they never do. And now he's used to it.

– How can he be a referee?

– He's completely sane. Except for this thing. It's like all his weirdness is contained in this. In you or me weirdness is spread out over everything. Half an inch of weirdness. Over everything. With him, it's just this one thing that's weird. Two foot deep.

– There's nothing weird about me.

– He doesn't drink. He is very fit. He's clear-headed. Seems very smart, intelligent. Do they make a lot of money?

– No. Referees? They're amateurs mate.

– They are not.

– Well. They get fees and that. I don't know really. I think most of them are schoolteachers or cops or something. There's that sergeant in Enfield is a Championship ref.

– Because he seems loaded. His place. His things. He likes nice things. He has about three computers. Art. Kitchen stuff. He has one of those high-tech kitchens. Takes about half an hour and seven different machines to make a cup of fucking coffee.

– This guy is not for you.

– He likes all the anti-referee stuff too. Seems to love the fact that he's hated. Likes travelling on his own. Hotel rooms. Driving up and down the country. Likes no one talking to him. Likes to show up and be really professional and eat on his own in the hotel and move on. He has languages. You know. Smart guy.

– Sees ghosts.

– Sees ghosts.

– I was doing a game in France. In Marseilles. Early round UEFA Cup match. This was a couple of years ago. It was the first time it happened. Second half. There was a stupid free-for-all in the centre circle after a bad tackle. Something like that happens, when there's shoulders charging in and a couple of mimsy head-butts, you stand back and watch. You let the captains sort it out, and you make a mental note of anyone who does any serious damage. So I'm standing back watching. I see one guy connect with a head. He's going. I see another guy spit. He spits but misses. He'll get a yellow. I see a lot of shouting and milling about and it's all just dumb and it calms down and eventually they all get the message because they see me standing there saying nothing. I call over the assistants to see if they've seen anything I've missed. And sure enough one of them has the head-butted guy bang to rights for an elbow which started the whole thing. So. That's fine. I call the captains over. I read them the riot act, I point out the three players I want, I red card the elbow and the head-butt, one from each team, that's fine, and I yellow card the spitter and he smiles at me and then I think I'm going to have to yellow card him again and send him off because he's taken his shirt off and I've only noticed and I don't have his number, and then the assistant and one of the captains are asking me to clarify who the yellow is for, and I'm saying that guy there, and then I realize, 'cos he's just smiling at me, that they can't see who the fuck I'm talking about, and that's it, first time. I've got one on the pitch.

– There's some people on the pitch. They think it's all over.

He didn't laugh. He put his hand to Hawthorn's throat.

– We need to move on, he said.

Johnson. Sheets. Rafsan.

– What is this?

– Oh shit. I forgot all about it.

– What is it?

– The Oyster Card guy. Rafsan.

Hawthorn was blank.

– Rafsan. You know. Murder in Crouch End. Last year. Rivers. So we need the worksheets from Finsbury Park. Johnson? In the station? BTP? What the hell is wrong with you?

– I remember.

– No you don't. You're completely clueless.

– OK. I think I must have been on leave or something. Should we go there now?

Child snapped his fingers a few times and pushed his glasses up his nose.

– No. After. We should probably expedite the suicide. And I want to do the paper on the paedo. And I need a shit.

They stood on the pavement outside the house and Hawthorn could still smell her. Her remains. He raised his hand to his mouth to discreetly sniff his sleeve. Child was watching him. He was on his mobile, talking to Frank Lenton. They were trying to work out whether Child should call Rivers.

– He'll call me. Frank. Frank. He'll call me if he wants to know anything. There's nothing ... Frank ... there's nothing to tell, anyway. She killed herself. Painfully. He's already seen anything I could tell him. No. No, Frank. You call him if you want. Jesus, Frank.

They found a patch of garden grass and stood on it and shuffled their feet back and forth and frowned at their shoes. Those bags are hopeless.

– You don't like that?
  – Not really, no.
  – Not at all?
  – No.
  – It's a trust thing.
  – No, it isn't. I just don't like it. It does nothing for me.

– OK.

– That's going to be a problem.

– Yes.

He left and came back. He went to the referee's flat and let himself in with a credit card. He sat at one of the computers and turned on bluetooth and turned on his phone and copied one of the pictures of the dead woman to the computer. Then he created a free email account and emailed the picture to the referee. With a message. Then he cleared all traces of it from the browser and securely deleted the picture. He went into the bedroom. There was no one there and the light was off and the bed was made. All these things that happened to other people. They were endless. A parade of disgusting things and he stood and watched it. Nothing ever happened to him.

He left the bedroom. He left the flat.

Nothing ever happened because no one ever heard about the things that happened.

– All that stuff about ghosts, seeing people, all that.

– Yeah.

– That was all a joke.

Hawthorn nodded.

– I knew that.

The referee looked at him.

– You have any stuff here?

– No. I'm good.

– OK. No hard feelings all right?

– Yeah. Absolutely.

– I'll see you around.

They drove towards Finsbury Park station.

– Rivers call?

– No. He was back in his office though.

They came out through the late afternoon light, a time that lasted nothing, and Child yawned and rubbed his eyes, and Hawthorn leaned into the passenger door.

– It's a set-up, said Child.

– What is?

– Every single fucking thing.

Hawthorn rang the bell and waited in the street looking at the first things. The sun was starting strong and it would be a good day. The air was fresh and warming, and there was a man running a cloth over a windscreen, and a woman at a window watching him, and there were a couple of teenagers jogging. He was fine. He was happy. This was happiness. It was morning and the sky was blue and he was very happy.

– What?

– Morning.

– What fucking time is it?

– Ten to nine.

The intercom rattled and sicked and the door hummed and he pushed it open. He wandered up the stairs with half a smile on his face. Child opened the door in a bathrobe, his bare chest and legs emerging like scoured ground. His glasses couldn't focus his eyes.

– Late night?

– Shut up. You're early.

– You want me to come back in ten minutes?

– We went clubbing. If you can imagine. Last time. Ever.

– Nothing ever happens to us, Child.

– No. Nothing ever does.

They opened the door on to the bus station and a man ran past.

He sat in the kitchen for a moment. He glanced at an old *Evening Standard*. He looked at the cork-board on the wall, at the photographs of Child and her, some postcards, a tube map, scribbled notes. They would want some breakfast. He looked in the fridge. He looked at the pots and pans. He opened a couple of cupboards. He stood and thought for a moment.

He filled the kettle, switched it on. He found a bowl. He took five eggs from the fridge and cracked them on the edge of the bowl. He found some skimmed milk and added a drop. Another drop. He twisted salt and pepper into the bowl. He took a fork and mixed. It made a ringing sound.

She appeared at the door. She looked a lot more clear-headed than Child.

– Hi, said Hawthorn.

– What are you doing?

– Breakfast. I thought you'd like some breakfast.

She just glared at him.

– You like eggs?

She walked off. Under the rising din of the kettle he heard voices in the bathroom.

He found butter in the fridge and put a knob in a pot, and put it on a medium gas ring and looked at it melting. There was bread in another cupboard. He stuck two slices in the toaster. When the butter had melted he poured in the milky eggs. He found a wooden spoon in a drawer and started stirring. His eyes looked for a teapot, plates, cups. Every so often he took a break from stirring and did something else. Buttered the first two slices of toast. Warmed the teapot. Put knives and forks on the table. Put out cups and teaspoons. Put out plates. He put more bread in the toaster. He filled the teapot. All the time stirring the eggs.

– What the fuck are you doing?

– Making breakfast.

– You trying to piss her off?

– No. Why? What's wrong?

– I don't fucking know, do I? Her kitchen.

He disappeared again.

Hawthorn stirred the eggs and frowned. Maybe she felt insulted. He comes in to their home. This faggot. This queer. Spends all day, all week, with her man, and here he comes first thing on a Sunday morning and wakes them from their bed, and he walks into their kitchen like he lives there.

— You making breakfast in my kitchen.

— I should have asked. Sorry.

She just looked at him.

— I thought you'd like it. That's all. I just thought it would be nice. You don't like eggs?

She shrugged. She was wearing Child's bathrobe. Or they had matching ones. She sat down.

— You want tea?

— Sure.

He poured her a mug of tea. Child appeared. Jeans and a T-shirt now.

— OK?

He sat down. Hawthorn put toast on plates and spooned the scrambled eggs on top. He put one in front of her. She just looked at it. He put one in front of Child. He nodded.

Hawthorn sat down. He had the smallest helping. The others said nothing about that but they noticed. They ate. They all ate. Child nodded. Nothing was said for a while. All they could hear was the world outside and their cutlery.

— Good, she said, eventually. Good eggs. Thank you.

Hawthorn nodded.

She looked at him and he didn't know how to look back.

— Cheer up, man, she said. It might never happen.

He closed his eyes and swallowed as slowly as he could.

This is a good morning, he kept telling himself. A good morning. Stop it.

– Sweet, said Child. Great eggs, Hawthorn.

He leaned across the table. Punched Hawthorn lightly on the arm.

– Just don't fucking do it again.

Hawthorn thought it was funny that no one laughed. They ate in silence and the windows rattled as a bus went by, and in the time they shared there was no time. No time at all. He could remember nothing of what had gone before, and he could think of no possible future.

And why did he never dream of this?